BELLA BALISTICA

AND THE AFRICAN SAFARI

ADAM GUILLAIN

Milet

Milet Publishing, LLC
333 North Michigan Avenue
Suite 530
Chicago, IL 60601
info@milet.com
www.milet.com

Bella Balistica and the African Safari
By Adam Guillain

Cover illustration by Sahin Erkocak

First published by Milet Publishing, LLC in 2006

ISBN-13: 978 1 84059 482 9
ISBN-10: 1 84059 482 9

Printed in Great Britain by Cox & Wyman

Please see our website www.milet.com for other **Bella Balistica** titles.

ABOUT THE AUTHOR

Adam Guillain was born into a family-run theatre school of nutters. He became a holiday-camp bluecoat before turning his hand to sports journalism, music and then teaching. After throwing it all in to live in a tropical rainforest and work with Zanzibari teachers for two years, he naturally turned his hand to novel writing! In 2005, Adam was appointed Writer in Residence at the Roald Dahl Museum and Story Centre in Great Missenden.

www.adam-guillain.co.uk

OTHER BELLA BALISTICA ADVENTURES

Bella Balistica and the Temple of Tikal
Bella Balistica and the Indian Summer

And for younger readers
Bella's Brazilian Football

For our beautiful daughter, Anna

AND THE AFRICAN SAFARI

"Throughout history, it has been the inaction of those who could have acted; the indifference of those who should have known better; the silence of the voice of justice when it mattered most; that has made it possible for evil to triumph."
Haile Selassie

"But if you know what they're doing is wrong you've got to speak out!" cried Bella. "Otherwise things just get worse!"
Bella Balistica and the African Safari

CHAPTER ONE

CAUGHT IN THE ACT

"I'm going to kill her," Bella panted as she leapt over yet another chimney pot and pounded her way across the icy slates.

"Get a grip," urged Bella's inner voice. "It's daylight – you're going to be seen."

In the sky, a solitary falcon peered down, surprised at the girl's lack of regard for enemy spies.

"She has a temper," thought the bird. "It will be her undoing."

The pursuit reminded Bella of her dramatic free-running escape from Diva Devaki over the rooftops of Delhi the previous summer; only this time, she was the one doing the chasing.

Coming up was another jump – this one the widest so far. Bella gripped her pendant firmly between her teeth and gathered her forces. The pendant, a gift from Bella's father to her mother on their wedding day, had been passed on to Bella through Bella's adoptive mum, Annie. Forged with glistening jewels into the image of Bella's animal twin – a resplendent Guatemalan quetzal bird – the pendant gave Bella extraordinary powers. She was about to leap when she slipped.

"Argh!" she cried as she tumbled down the roof. She made a frantic grab for the gutter and missed.

"You're so dead," said her inner voice, flatly.

But Bella's skills were getting sharper by the day. With only centimetres to spare before hitting the ground, she turned herself into her animal twin and flew up into the air.

"So it's true," smirked the falcon, circling down for a closer look at the colourful quetzal bird that wonderously metamorphosed in place of the girl. This was the final piece of evidence he needed. "So the human child our enemy prophesied has finally come," he thought. "Too bad she's going to disappoint them."

Bella had been half-aware of the falcon's presence but was too preoccupied with the chase to consider the danger it posed. Seconds later, she was back in her human form, tracking her target as it darted under the axles of a lorry grinding its way up Shooters Hill. Bella slammed the palm of her hand against the lorry's door and ran out into road. Against a barrage of horns from angry motorists, Bella made it to the other side of the road.

"I'm reporting you!" shouted the lorry driver, rolling down his window. "Use the crossing!"

Bella had successfully kept her powers under wraps for almost a year and was getting complacent. If the driver had been a bit less concerned with the traffic, he might have seen her miraculous transformation from a quetzal bird back into a schoolgirl. As it was, he could see by her uniform that she was from Crown Woods Secondary School and he was already on his mobile phone to the headteacher.

Using the power of the pendant, Bella closed her eyes and centred all her energies on picking out the sound she was after. "Got you!" she thought, clenching her fists. The sound of scampering paws bounding through flowerbeds and hedges was already several hundred metres away. Determined not to be outwitted, she sprang onto a garden wall and scoured the suburban landscape.

Over the past few weeks, Bella had honed her ability to focus and magnify an image as if she were looking through binoculars. Within a few seconds, her target was in her sights.

"Prudence!" she bellowed, jumping down from the wall and breaking into a sprint across the gardens.

When Bella eventually emerged from a bush by the main road, several people gave her a critical glance. Her uniform was filthy and her long black hair was speckled with berries and tiny twigs.

"Come here!" she ordered the terrified cat as it leapt off a bin onto the long wall by the railway line. Trespassing here was strictly prohibited, but still Bella jumped, her arms and legs flying wildly in the air before she landed rather precariously on top of the wall.

"Alright, pig-face!" someone yelled from a passing car.

Bella lost her concentration and shot a look over her shoulder.

It was a mistake.

CHAPTER TWO

BELLA'S BETRAYAL

Bella heard the crack of her arm as she used it to break her fall.

"Ahhh!" she cried. The pain was excruciating.

Eugene Briggs was with his mum on the morning school run. Eugene had a history of bullying, particularly towards Bella, but what really infuriated Bella this morning was how his mum allowed him to call her 'pig-face' so openly. The landrover pulled over.

"Aren't you going to tell him off?" Bella hollered as Eugene and his mother got out.

"Tell him off for what, dear?" asked Mrs Briggs calmly, waddling around to the kerb.

Bella was a little taken aback by Mrs Briggs' appearance.

"She looks like she's been locked away for years," she thought, observing Mrs Briggs' white, craggy skin. "Like one of her husband's old relics." Mysteriously, no one had seen Bella's nemesis, Professor Ted Briggs, for months. Bella was trying to remember the last time she'd actually seen his wife. "It must have been when she used to drop Eugene off at the Hawksmore nursery," she decided. "And that was seven years ago!"

Even now, Bella recalled that everything Mrs Briggs wore reeked of cigars and looked weird. Today, Mrs Briggs was wearing a big, baggy black dress and thick brown tights. If

Bella hadn't been in such pain she might have laughed. But as if to add insult to injury, Prudence, the murderous tabby Bella had just spent the best part of half an hour trying to catch, was now purring down at her from the top of the wall.

"I'm not finished with you yet," Bella growled through gritted teeth as she quickly tried to use the pendant to heal her injuries. But there was no time.

"I think you've broken your arm," said Mrs Briggs in a matter-of-fact way, observing from a great height how Bella's arm hung in the wrong direction from the joint. "We need to get you to the hospital."

"No," Bella grimaced. "I'll be fine, really. I can make my own way . . ."

"We wouldn't hear of it," Eugene interrupted with mock sympathy. "You need seeing to." He brushed back his floppy blond fringe and gave Bella a wicked grin. "Didn't I say Bella was a bit . . . strange?" he asked his mum gleefully.

"You did, darling," she replied, narrowing her eyes. "Almost . . .," she paused for a moment, trying to gauge which word might best offend, ". . . freakish. It's a wonder anyone adopted her at all." The sourness in Mrs Briggs' voice made Bella squirm. She realized now that while Eugene got his tall, lanky features from his father, his slitty eyes and venomous tongue definitely came from his mum.

Since Bella's adventure in India last summer, the feud between Bella and Eugene had worsened. The only thing holding Eugene back since they'd started secondary school was the fact that he was little more than a bullying minnow compared with the mighty sharks higher up in school.

"You wait till he gets to Year Eight," Bella had told her

best friend, Charlie Stevens, the other night. "There'll be no stopping him."

Charlie's real name was Charlotte, but only her mum and dad called her that. Her mum ran the trendy hair and beauty salon on Eltham High Street.

"Let me help you," said Eugene, gripping Bella's good arm tightly and yanking her up. Distracted by the pain, Bella's resistance was easily quashed when Mrs Briggs also weighed in with unnecessary force. Before Bella knew it, she'd been pushed into the back of the landrover and they were off.

"I need to get these broken bones healed," thought Bella, seething with anger. But it was impossible. Eugene kept staring at her neck, almost willing her to use the pendant and expose her powers.

"Let me call her mum," said Eugene, dipping quickly into his mother's handbag for her mobile phone.

"You are thoughtful, dear," said Mrs Briggs. "Make sure you tell her exactly what her little darling was up to."

"I'll do the talking, if you don't mind," said Bella crossly, reaching out for the phone with her left hand.

"Oh no you don't," hissed Eugene, recoiling quickly. He got Bella's number from directory enquiries. "Seems like you're the only Balistica in London," he grinned as the operator made the connection.

Bella's mum worked as a midwife at Greenwich Hospital. "It's her day off!" Bella panicked. To Bella's relief, she heard her mum's answering machine message.

"Good morning, *Mizz* Balistica," Eugene started after the beep, "I'm afraid I have some bad news . . ."

Mrs Briggs drove them straight to accident and emergency.

In no time at all Bella had seen a consultant and had been referred to a radiologist for an x-ray.

"I'm afraid I'm going to have to mention this to the headteacher," Mrs Briggs told Bella while they waited for the results. "It's for your own good, you understand?"

Bella could hear her mum running up the corridor from fifty metres. Wearing a smart leather jacket and black jeans, Annie arrived as the radiologist emerged with the x-ray results in a large brown envelope.

"Bella, are you alright?" Annie panted. "I was in the shower when Eugene left his kind message." She put her arms carefully around her daughter's shoulders and gave her a kiss. "You bolted out the front door so early this morning you didn't even say goodbye," she gently scolded.

"I'm fine," Bella squirmed, ashamed of her mum's affections in front of Eugene and his mum. But it was about to get worse.

"Bella," said Annie, a little more sternly, "what do we need to say to Eugene and his mother? Poor Eugene is late for school on your account."

"And it's our maths test this morning," Eugene interjected forlornly. "I revised for hours."

Bella withered under Annie's glare. She'd been allowed to spend the whole evening playing in the attic because she'd told her mum there was no homework.

"Bella . . .?" prompted Annie, implying she was ready to hear Bella's defence.

Bella was so furious, she was shaking. "There's no way I'm apologizing to him," she muttered, clenching her fists.

"She's embarrassed," said Mrs Briggs in a sickly-sweet voice. "Perhaps she'll thank me another time."

"Oh, she will," said Annie firmly.

Eugene's face turned a bright beetroot colour as he fought to suppress his laughter. By the time he and his mum had reached the automatic doors, the corridor was reverberating with their hysterical guffaws.

"Can't you see what they're like?" Bella thundered.

"I don't care," Annie told her. "It's you I'm worried about."

Bella was bursting with rage. She yearned that her mystical powers could summon up a mighty storm and strike the Briggs' landrover with lightning. The rumble of thunder that followed might have been an ominous sign as to how far-reaching Bella's skills had become had it not been for the rollicking she was getting from her mum.

"You can forget watching football on telly this week," Annie told her. "And you're grounded. I want you home by four every day for a month." The sound of torrential rain began to pound against the windows.

"But that's not fair!" Bella shouted as a flash of lightning caused the lights to flicker.

The whole thing was a complete disaster. By eleven o'clock Bella's arm was in plaster and hanging from a sling. Not only was she going to be out of action for playing football until well into the new year, she was also going to miss representing the school at next week's fencing finals. Since starting after-school classes in September, Bella had become quite a rising star in less than three months.

"Best raw talent I've ever seen in a sword fighter," her teacher, Mr Arrivalo, had told her mum. "If only I could persuade her to give up football and concentrate on her fencing, she could be County Champion before the year's out."

Bella really enjoyed the mental discipline of the sport; centring her body and focusing her mind on visualizing every combination of parry and riposte she could use to turn the match her way. She was particularly proud of herself, because never once had she used the power of the pendant to enhance her performance. From the very first time she held a sword, Bella had felt at one with her blade.

"You really fancy yourself as a bit of a Zorro, don't you?" Charlie would tease, knowing how well her friend loved to see films with furious sword fights set in medieval fortresses. The only thing Bella didn't like about these films was the fact that the brave, sword-wielding knights were always men.

Whenever she fenced, Bella imagined herself defying gravity, scaling walls and performing incredible acrobatic leaps to defeat whole legions of warriors. It was unbearable to think that because of Eugene Briggs, she was going to miss the chance to show off her fencing skills in competition.

Annie let Bella spend the rest of the afternoon resting on the sofa watching television.

"I had probably better stay home for the rest of the week," Bella suggested hopefully.

The very next day Bella found herself having to sit through an hour-long assembly about the dangers of freerunning and playing by the railway track. This was followed by a patronizing lecture on how to cross the road after a phone complaint from a lorry driver on Shooters Hill. On top of that, Bella had five straight detentions to get through as a punishment for trespassing on railway property and bringing the school into disrepute.

"And all because of that stupid cat!" Bella complained to Charlie that break-time.

"Did she leave another dead sparrow on the patio?" asked Charlie.

"It was a robin," Bella replied. "She does it to annoy me."

"Bella, that's stupid," said Charlie. "Cats don't do things to make humans mad. They act on instinct. If you didn't feed her, she'd have to kill them to eat and stay alive. It's how nature works."

"I don't feed her," said Bella haughtily. "If it were up to me I'd board up the cat flap and send her packing." With a quetzal for an animal twin, Bella was instinctively suspicious of cats.

The two friends were finishing their break-time drink when Charlie gave Bella a sharp nudge with her elbow.

"Bella, look," she hushed sharply, gesturing to the blond Year Eight boy she fancied as he strode purposefully towards them. "Isn't he gorgeous?"

Bella groaned. She found Charlie's growing preoccupation with boys irritating.

"Hey, Mickey," smiled Charlie, with a flick of her silky-red hair.

Charlie's blue, twinkly eyes and brown freckles made her easily the prettiest girl in Year Seven in Bella's view – especially now that she was growing her hair long. She was popular with the other girls because she was chatty and friendly and always willing to help them with their schoolwork. Few boys ever took advantage of Charlie's willingness to explain things. They were more interested in who she fancied.

"How's it going?" Charlie asked Mickey.

Charlie's blushes alone completely exposed her feelings. Mickey's tall, broad-shouldered frame and blond, blue-eyed looks had made many of the girls gush since his arrival three weeks ago. Not Bella. She almost gagged at the lingering smell of his shampoo and fancy deodorants. Even more a cause for concern was the fact that whenever Bella saw him, her pendant turned cold, a sure sign that there were things about him to distrust.

"I'm sorry about your arm, Bella," said Mickey, blanking Charlie's question and turning his attention to Bella's sling. Like many children at Bella's new school, Mickey spoke with an overseas accent.

"It's nothing," said Bella, averting her eyes from Mickey's gaze. "At least I have an excuse not to write neatly for six weeks."

Actually, Bella had already healed her arm using the power of the pendant, but knew full well she would have to keep it in the sling and plaster for fear of raising suspicion.

"Mickey," Charlie interrupted, taking his hand and slipping him a small scrap of paper with her mobile number on it. "Send me a text. Mum says I can go ice-skating on Saturday. Maybe you'd like to come." Bella felt embarrassed by Charlie's forwardness in the face of such indifference.

"Why doesn't she ask me if I want to go skating?" Bella wondered, feeling a little hurt that Charlie wanted to spend time with Mickey rather than with her. Bella found it confusing that her best friend was changing and becoming interested in different things.

The bell rang for the end of break and Bella and Charlie headed off for their geography lesson.

"Meet me after football," called Mickey, tying his hair back with a thick elastic band. "I'll walk you both home."

"He's so good-looking," Charlie giggled as they tried to side-step the inevitable pushing and shoving of the older children through the corridors. "What do you think?"

"I think he needs a haircut," said Bella dismissively. "I thought long hair was against the rules."

"Do you think he'll text?" asked Charlie, undeterred.

"No," said Bella curtly. "And if I was you, I wouldn't give it a second thought. He's not good enough for you."

"Oh come on, Bella," Charlie moaned, "stop being such a bore and try and have a bit of fun."

Harsh words between the two friends were becoming more frequent. Despite having a reputation for toughness, Bella was hurt by Charlie's rebuke. "I am good fun," she thought. "And I'm not the one being a complete and utter bore."

But Charlie and Bella had a long history of friendship, and despite her reservations Bella really wished Mickey would give Charlie a call. Since her mum and dad had split up, Charlie was finding life quite tough.

"I just want things to be normal again," she would sob to Bella when things were really getting her down. "Why do adults make things so horrible and complicated?"

Bella found the geography lesson with Mrs Tinker really gripping. It was all about climate change and the effects of global warming on different regions of the world. Mrs Tinker took them to the computer suite and divided them into pairs to research areas of the world with a history of famine.

"Perhaps a good starting point would be to investigate

which crops or businesses your country is best known for," Mrs Tinker suggested. "Then consider how these might be affected by climate change."

Bella and Charlie had been given Ethiopia and quickly discovered that Ethiopia's economy depended almost entirely on the success of its coffee crop. This was a problem because the crops were ruined sometimes when the rains failed to come. Recently, a rise in average temperatures and a fall in world coffee prices had caused the Ethiopian people great hardship.

"My mum buys Ethiopian coffee," said Bella, typing 'fair trade' into the site search with her left hand. "She says it's important because it gives power to local communities and helps them survive if they have a poor harvest."

With her right hand in plaster, Bella found typing frustrating and so Charlie took over. They quickly discovered that if the big coffee companies kept forcing Ethiopian producers to lower their prices, the economy would collapse.

At dinnertime, Bella and Charlie took their sandwiches to the dinner hall.

"I hate the smell in here, don't you?" said Charlie. "It's so cabbagey."

But Bella's mind was still thinking about the last lesson.

"It makes me so angry," she told Charlie as she unwrapped her sandwich. "To think that wealthy corporations will squeeze every last penny from people working so hard to make a living. It isn't fair!"

"That's such a Bella thing to say," Charlie sighed.

Bella found Charlie's tone difficult to understand. Usually Charlie was more supportive of the way she felt about things.

"All I can think about is my dad and when he's coming

back to see me," said Charlie.

Bella, too, often felt wretched when she thought about her own father and what he was up to.

"I can't see my mum and dad ever getting back together now," said Charlie, with tears in her eyes. Bella took her friend's hand and gave it a gentle squeeze.

"And I can't see my adoptive mum and my birthfather even living in the same country," thought Bella, feeling as torn as ever by her feelings towards them. "That kind of thing doesn't happen."

As soon as they could, Bella and Charlie were outside on the playground watching football. Bella was gutted she couldn't join in.

"You can still have a game," she told Charlie.

"Nah," said Charlie. "I'll keep you company."

"You just want to gawk at your boyfriend," Bella teased.

And that's exactly what happened. Even Bella had to admit that the way Mickey could mesmerize defenders with his amazing footwork, and pass the ball with such precision, was exciting to watch.

"He's a classy player," she told Charlie.

"You'd better watch out, Bella," Charlie replied. "He's a master sword-fighter too, apparently."

The afternoon was so tedious Bella gave up on Mrs Dubock's English lesson and focused instead on the classroom clock. The Quetzal had demonstrated such incredible powers in controlling time during Bella's previous adventures that she was determined to acquire the skill herself. "You'll learn," the bird had teased her. "In time."

"What are you doing?" Charlie hushed. Bella's face was

bright red, her brow was furrowed and her whole body was shaking with determination as she stared at the clock. "It looks like you're trying to lay an egg."

Bella burst out laughing.

"Fifty lines tomorrow at break-time, Bella Balistica," ordered Mrs Dubock, affronted by Bella's interruption. "And I think I'd better have a word with your mother."

"But I can't write, Miss," said Bella cheekily, pointing to her injured arm.

"You can write with your foot for all I care," replied Mrs Dubock. "It will give *me* something to laugh about."

After school it was football training on the playing fields with a guest coach from Bella's favourite team, Charlton Athletic. Even though she couldn't play herself, Bella had been furious when she found out that the first session was for boys only.

"Why can't we have mixed sessions?" she'd complained to her new form teacher, Mr Appleby. "It's not fair!"

"An attitude like that is going to get you into a great deal of trouble," was the only reply she got.

Bella and Charlie sat down to watch the boys train from the sidelines. Charlie was quickly rooting through her bag for her mobile.

"Let's see if he's texted yet," she said hopefully. Bella glanced at the clutter inside Charlie's bag.

"I thought you already had an MP3 player," she said, noticing Charlie's brand new iPod.

"Another present from my dad," said Charlie. "I think he feels guilty."

Charlie gave her friend a pitying look.

"You haven't got a mobile phone and you haven't got a boyfriend," Charlie told Bella. "Round here, that makes you a bit of a freak."

Bella found it embarrassing that her mum didn't let her have her own mobile phone.

"If you're going to flirt with boys, a mobile phone is a must," said Charlie. But Bella wasn't interested in the flirting. She was more into the idea of getting text updates on football scores. She knew a mobile phone would be yet another way Eugene Briggs could harass her, but she still would have liked one. Unlike some of the other children who were sent mean texts, Bella saw having a phone as an opportunity to collect evidence and expose the bullies.

The girls returned to watching the boys train. The session was rigorous and many of them, including Eugene Briggs and fellow gang member, Conner Mitchell, were clearly flagging – some even had to stop to use their inhalers. Mickey, however, was doing splendidly.

"Who's that tall black boy?" asked Charlie. "He's the only one who can give Mickey a run for his money."

"His name's Leeyio," said Bella. "His family is from Kenya."

One of the things Bella really loved about coming to a big city school was meeting children from different backgrounds. It made her feel less of a freak for being the only Guatemalan pupil there.

"Mickey's got great technique," said Bella admiringly. "And he's very fit."

"See, you do like him," Charlie teased.

"Nah," said Bella. "He lets Eugene Briggs hang around him too much for my liking."

"Come on, Bella, get yourself a boyfriend," said Charlie. "Even Imogen Meeks has one."

The fact that one of Bella's own friends was now going out with Roland 'The Rat' Richardson was more a cause for concern than excitement to Bella – especially as Roland used to be in Eugene's gang.

Since starting secondary school, many of the girls in Bella's year-group had become obsessed with getting a boyfriend. Even without Charlie's blunt reminder it made Bella feel awkward that she was more interested in football and adventures than kissing boys. Sometimes the pressure of needing to be like everyone else got Bella down.

"Maybe I'll get a boyfriend soon," she replied, hoping to appease Charlie. But she didn't feel convinced.

Bella and Charlie met Mickey by the school gates after the session. He was the last boy out and looked fresh-faced and well-groomed after his shower.

"Mickey's last school was in New York," Charlie whispered as he approached.

"How do you know so much about him?" Bella asked in a hushed voice.

"When you fancy someone, Bella, you get to know everything," Charlie told her. "You can't help yourself. It's too exciting."

"Be careful you don't come across as desperate," Bella warned. "If you do, he'll never treat you with any respect."

"You were great," Charlie gushed as soon as Mickey was in range. "Easily the best player there."

Bella sighed to herself.

"How's your arm, Bella?" asked Mickey, totally blanking

Charlie. "I hear you're going to be out of fencing action for most of the season. I was looking forward to a match with a worthy adversary."

Bella felt the cold warning tingles from the pendant. She'd heard about Mickey's talent for fencing but had never seen him in action. She had, however, observed him in the library one lunchtime pouring over a book about medieval knights. Even at a glance, she could see that some of the images were bloody. Mickey had left the book out on the table when he went for lunch and Bella was quick to get her hands on it. She discovered that Mickey had been reading all about a band of warriors called the Knights Templar, and soon found herself gripped by the legends surrounding their renowned adventures.

"I won't be out of action for that long," said Bella, wiggling the fingers at the end of her injured arm. "It's feeling better already. You two have a leisurely walk. I should have been home half an hour ago." Bella slipped her arm out of its sling and started to jog off. She'd only stayed to keep Charlie company while she waited for Mickey.

"Great idea," said Mickey. "Let's all run."

Bella found Mickey's decision to run alongside her intensely irritating. She knew Charlie was desperate to get to talk with Mickey on her own, but she couldn't shake him off. Before she knew it, she and Mickey were saying goodbye to Charlie at her house and running off together up Shooters Hill.

"I thought you lived near Eltham High Street," Bella panted when Charlie was out of earshot. Her pendant was starting to feel cold again.

"I do," he replied.

"Then . . ." Bella started, before Mickey reached out and

grabbed her hand. Shocked by his advances, Bella stopped running and turned to look up into his face.

"What's it like, not having a dad?" he asked with a grin. Bella tried to push him away with her left arm. "Why didn't he look after you when your mother died?" he added.

Mickey stared into Bella's eyes, willing her anger to rise.

"Back off!" said Bella, clenching her fists. As soon as Bella had started to believe her father was alive, this was the question that hurt her the most. It still did.

"Hey, calm down," said Mickey, reaching out to pat Bella's shoulder only to get a sharp slap on the wrist.

"I'm not joking, Mickey – back off!" Bella warned.

Bella's volatile nature was well-known and yet still Mickey continued to goad her. It was as if he were trying to probe away at a weakness that he could exploit. Her pendant was so ice-cold now it hurt.

"Why so fiery?" asked Mickey teasingly, staring with some suspicion at Bella's plaster-cast arm.

Bella looked up into Mickey's strong, handsome face. His icy-blue eyes were staring so intensely into hers it was scary.

"Beware," urged a familiar voice inside her head.

An unnerving tingling sensation shot down her spine, covering her in goose bumps and numbing any thought she had of retreat. And then, with more confidence than Bella thought possible, Mickey swept back his long blond hair, yanked her towards him and kissed her on the lips. Bella panicked. Her thoughts shot straight to Charlie. "You're betraying your best friend," she told herself. But something about the moment was so electric she couldn't resist.

CHAPTER THREE

THE PORTRAIT

By the time Bella got back to 14 Birdcage Crescent it was almost five o'clock.

"Charlie mustn't find out I kissed Mickey," she thought. "She'll never forgive me." In her panic, Bella was forgetting how damaging secrets could be. Both she and Charlie had kept the bullying antics of Eugene Briggs under wraps because they were terrified things would only get worse if they spoke out. As it turned out, things had gotten worse anyway.

She tried to slip her key into the front door, hoping she might sneak upstairs and make out she'd been home for a while.

"So, you come home eventually then." Annie was standing in the hall in her midwife's uniform with her arms firmly crossed. "I had Mrs Dubock on the phone to me at the hospital this afternoon, telling me how rude you were in her lesson."

"But Mum," Bella pleaded, "I was only . . ."

"Later," said Annie, before Bella could get into her stride. "Right now I want you to go to your room and tidy it up. It's a disgrace!"

The day was getting worse by the minute. Bella dragged herself up the stairs, went to her room and quickly discarded her sling. The incident with Mickey had been very confusing. On top of that, she was in trouble yet again at school and with her mum.

"I'm never speaking to that boy again," she resolved, gathering up the clothes on the floor and thrusting them into any drawer she could find with space for them. When the room was free of surface debris, Bella changed into her jeans and red Charlton Athletic football top and slumped down on the edge of her bed. "I wish you were here, Father," she whispered.

Bella thought about her father everyday. She'd never accepted the story of his death in a Guatemalan earthquake. Over the years she had collected an album full of articles about a man called Eduardo Salvatore – the Guatemalan football coach who saved her life at Heathrow Airport last summer – and was convinced that he was her father. She closed her eyes and tried to visualize herself sitting by her father's side and was rather surprised when his image appeared, sitting cross-legged by an open fire and drinking from a small cup. The second he seemed to sense her presence he looked up and smiled at her. The moment was so vivid to Bella it felt real.

"Why are you always so far away?" Bella asked as the image slowly dissolved before her. She thumped her duvet with her fists and stomped downstairs.

Bella found Annie sitting on the sofa watching the news and went to join her, hoping to catch the sports segment. Bella was bored at first to find the news was all about the run-up to next week's summit meeting of world leaders in New York.

"On the agenda as usual," the newscaster was saying, "the rise in global warming, aid to the developing world and fair trade."

"About time," said Annie, kicking off her shoes. Bella soon

found herself becoming interested in the report.

"Business representatives from the world's most powerful company, The Corporation, met world leaders today in the final day of lobbying over the wording of critical new trade agreements," the announcer continued.

"You think it's the politicians we elect who are running the world," said Annie. "But really, it's business leaders. When are they going to stop destroying the environment and ripping off the developing world?"

Bella hated the sense of powerlessness she felt whenever she thought about such things. "They never listen to children anyway," she thought. "They decide what's best for the rich countries and do it regardless of what anyone thinks!"

Annie reached for the remote and switched the television off in disgust.

"Right then," she started, turning her attention to her troubled daughter. The phone rang.

"I'll get it," said Bella.

She ran to the phone and picked up. Before Bella had time to work out what was happening, Charlie was off.

"Why didn't you tell me you fancied him?" Charlie sobbed. Bella had barely said hello.

"What do you mean?" Bella stammered. The second she asked the question, Bella knew she'd made a mistake.

"Oh, Bella, I thought we didn't have secrets between us," Charlie blurted. "I know all about it. Roland Richardson saw you snogging him on Shooters Hill. He texted Imogen and she called me."

"Charlie, I'm so sorry," said Bella, with a lump in her throat. "It all happened so quickly, I . . ." But Charlie had already hung up the phone.

Bella was in shock. She stood with the phone to her ear for almost a minute before Annie came over and put her arm around her shoulder.

"Bella, what's wrong?" she asked kindly. Bella wriggled free from her mum's embrace and stormed up to the attic while Annie sank with despair into the chair by the phone.

Without waiting for the fluorescent light to flicker on, Bella made her way over to the hammock and pulled herself in. Throwing herself face down into the musty old pillow, she started giving it a real beating with her fists.

"What was I doing?" she sobbed to herself. "I just folded. It was like I actually wanted him to kiss me." The idea that she'd betrayed her friend was so repulsive, Bella felt sick. Even without looking, she knew the old portrait that hung from a rusty nail on the far wall was giving her a fierce glare.

"I knew Mickey was bad news," she chastised herself. "No wonder the pendant always turned cold whenever I saw him."

"The boy knows about your powers," whispered a familiar voice.

Bella believed this voice to be that of Itzamna, the beautiful Mayan goddess in the painting. The portrait often spoke to Bella like an inner voice, advising and comforting her – as well as telling her off.

"But he can't," Bella pleaded. "I haven't told anyone."

"Put aside the fact you're chasing cats over rooftops in broad daylight and flying around as a quetzal almost every night of the week – there are all the myths," the voice inside her head went on. "There are more prophesies about you than you could possibly imagine – now for goodness sake, get a grip!"

Bella knew she'd been a bit careless recently, but she was sure no one had ever seen her doing anything so out-of-the-ordinary they might be on to her. "Maybe if I could turn back time, I could push Mickey away when he reached out to kiss me and none of this would ever have happened," she pondered, reaching under her blouse for the pendant.

"You're not ready for that yet," said the voice. "You need to love, learn, forgive and move on."

Bella was a little sick of the portrait always harping on about this. She slipped off the pendant and raised it up to the light. The multi-coloured gems looked as spectacular as ever and made her feel incredibly proud.

"You must have looked so beautiful in this, Mother," thought Bella, turning to hold the pendant up to the portrait. For a moment she allowed herself to fantasize that the woman in the painting was her birthmother. She imagined how happy her mother and father must have been on their wedding day when they exchanged their necklaces as gifts. "Thanks for passing the pendant on to me, Mother," she said to herself.

Along with a beautifully hand-carved jewellery box, Bella's mother had given the pendant to Annie to give to Bella in the event of her death. Annie was working at the time as a volunteer at the Santa Maria orphanage in Quetzaltenango and, as fate would have it, she was the delivering midwife at Bella's birth. The experience had been so moving to Annie that after the mother's tragic death, Annie adopted her spirited baby. Somehow, though, between Guatemala and London the pendant had mysteriously gone astray. It turned up last Christmas when Bella found it inside a secret compartment within her jewellery box. She soon discovered that the pendant possessed powers beyond her wildest dreams. With it, not only could she transform herself and fly as a quetzal, and speak every human and animal language in the world, but she was also gaining an increasing sense of connection with her mystical past. The only pendant Bella had ever seen that was as beautiful as her own was the jaguar pendant worn by her birthfather.

Like Bella and every other person in the world, Bella's father had an animal twin – a nahual – born into the world at the exact same moment as its human counterpart. Both human and nahual shared the same characteristics and were destined to look out for one another. Bella had first seen her father and his pendant when their paths crossed over the summer at Heathrow airport. For a short while her father's pendant had been lost to him, but luckily Bella managed to grab it and escape, hiding it safely away in her jewellery box along with her own. The night her father came to collect it, he spoke to Bella as if in a dream.

"I love you, Bella," he whispered. "I want to take you with me now, but I can't. But please, don't feel sad. Everything's going to be alright."

When Bella woke up, the jaguar pendant had gone.

"When's my father coming back?" asked Bella now, turning to face the portrait. "Tell me something useful for a change."

The events at Heathrow airport had only made Bella more convinced than ever that she and her father would be together one day. But there had been no word from her father since, and now she was in more trouble at home and at school than she'd ever been. On top of everything, she'd fallen out with Charlie.

"I'm giving my powers a rest," she told herself, slipping the pendant off and swinging herself out of the hammock. "It's not as if they're doing me any good."

She made her way to the old wooden chest, covered with beautifully-carved pictures of jaguars and tropical birds, and threw the lid open. Delving through all her mum's travel souvenirs, she searched for her jewellery box. "Here it is," she thought, taking it out and turning the ingenious sequence of drawer handles that unlocked its secret compartment.

As Bella understood it, all her powers came directly from the pendant itself. Without the pendant, she was no more than an ordinary twelve-year-old girl.

"Some help you were today," she sighed, dropping it into the secret space.

Suddenly there was an excruciating shriek, followed by a sharp hammering on the skylight.

CHAPTER FOUR

GREAT NEWS

"Quetzal?" thought Bella.

She jumped onto the chest and pushed the skylight open. There, to her relief, was the resplendent bird who had already seen her through two perilous adventures in Guatemala and India.

"You need a bath," said Bella, brushing the soot from the Quetzal's emerald green feathers.

"Don't talk to me about the pollution," spat the Quetzal. "There are so many oil refineries and power stations these days, I hardly stand a chance with all the air miles I tot up. The world's not a place for frequent fliers any more." The great bird gave his wings a big shakeout then started to preen his fiery red feathers. "When are you humans going to realize what you're doing to the planet? The biggest challenge of your generation, and no one cares two hoots."

"I care," Bella objected. "None of this is my fault, you know. It's just hard knowing what to do about it."

"I suppose you either walk or cycle everywhere you go," said the Quetzal sarcastically. "I bet you write letters to the Prime Minister weekly and never leave lights on around the house." The Quetzal could see that Bella was lost for words. "You're like everyone else," he told her, hammering his argument home with a self-righteous flick of his beak. "Can't be bothered!" Invigorated by his verbal assault, the Quetzal turned to matters closer to hand. "Hey – and what's with that falcon I can see stalking your house?" he asked. "It's murder out there, what with all the ravens and crows knocking around as well."

Over the last few weeks Bella had also noticed a sharp increase in such birds. Twice now she'd been chased home by a vicious falcon intent on biting her tail.

"Are you going to invite me in, or what?" asked the Quetzal, tapping his foot. "It's not exactly tropical out here."

"Come on then," said Bella warmly, stepping aside to let him in. The Quetzal dropped through the skylight and came to rest on one of the lower rafters.

"A little bird told me about your accident," he tutted, casting a critical eye over Bella's arm. "How come it's still in plaster?"

"Forget my arm," said Bella crossly. "Where on earth have you been? I haven't seen you for weeks."

"Business trip," replied the Quetzal haughtily, flying down to perch on one of the rafters. "While you've been showing off your powers to the entire neighbourhood, I've been . . ."

"Wait a minute!" Bella interrupted. "I can understand what you're saying!" Bella had never heard the bird speak without the aid of her pendant before.

"Well, stone the crows!" squawked the Quetzal. "The girl's a genius!"

"But how?" asked Bella. The Quetzal gave her a disbelieving glare.

"Can you ride a bike?" he asked, trying to rally a little patience.

Bella was confused.

"Yes," she nodded cautiously, not entirely sure that the Quetzal was going to answer her question.

"And do you ride it with stabilizers on?" the Quetzal continued, anxious to make his point.

"Of course not!" Bella shouted.

"Well, there you go," replied the Quetzal triumphantly. "Another lesson, perfectly delivered. I really am an excellent teacher."

Bella found the Quetzal's pedantic tone highly annoying but there was too much on her mind to pick a fight now.

"You mean I don't need the pendant to use my powers any more?" she asked in disbelief. The Quetzal looked concerned.

"What kind of grades are you getting at school?" he asked.

"Stop talking to me like I'm an idiot!" Bella retorted. The Quetzal screwed up his face and shrugged his shoulders.

"And you're the great hope for the future," he mumbled, shaking his head forlornly.

"Bella, are you alright up there?" called Annie. "Dinner's ready in five minutes."

Annie had decided to give Bella a bit of space and talk to her later. It was a strategy she'd learnt paid off with her fiery and passionate daughter.

"Okay, Mum," replied Bella.

"You go and have your dinner," chirped the Quetzal, flying up to the skylight. "I've only popped by to tell you that I'm to take you to your father as soon as I've finished shoring up support for the big summit meeting he's planning."

"You've seen him!" cried Bella. "Then where is he?"

The Quetzal paused. "He's waiting for us in a small village by the shores of Lake Tana in Ethiopia," he said finally. "But don't even think about finding it on your own. It's the back of beyond, believe me."

"How is he?" Bella demanded. "And what's this summit meeting all about?" The Quetzal gestured with his wings for Bella to hush.

"There are dark forces gathering and we need to be swift," he whispered.

"Then we must leave now!" Bella insisted as loudly as ever. The Quetzal stared Bella straight in the eye.

"Whatever you do – don't leave without me," he told her. "I'll be back in a few days and then I'll want you ready with your pendant, raring to go." He flew up through the skylight onto the roof.

"I thought I didn't need my pendant any more," said Bella.

"Not for the easy stuff," chirped the Quetzal, poking his head down through the hatch. "Any idiot can fly." The Quetzal looked at his pupil with the eye of a teacher desperate for the long summer holidays.

"But you can play such wonderful tricks with time," Bella complained. "Can't you hurry things along a bit?"

"If it's a magician you're after, call Harry Potter," snapped the Quetzal, opening his wings.

Before Bella knew it the Quetzal was gone. She sank down onto the Guatemalan chest and stared blankly at the floor.

"I have a rotten day when absolutely everything goes wrong, and now this!" she groaned. The news that she was about to be taken to meet her father had been so cruelly dangled before her and then whisked away – it felt like the final straw. Closing her eyes for a moment, Bella tried again to picture herself by her father's side. At first there was just the sense of his powerful aura. She tried to find him but instead was disorientated by images of flickering shadows inside a cramped, gloomy room.

"I can't wait!" she thought, jumping up.

Consumed with guilt, not only about upsetting Charlie but the promise she was about to break with the Quetzal, Bella gave the plaster on her arm a whack against a beam, cracked it open and ripped it off.

Within five minutes of the Quetzal's departure, Bella was flicking through her atlas to find Lake Tana. As soon as she'd plotted herself a route she retrieved the pendant from her jewellery box.

Transforming herself into her animal twin, Bella flew up through the skylight and headed off in a southeasterly direction out of London towards the coast.

"Don't worry, Father," she whispered into the wind. "I'm coming."

CHAPTER FIVE

THE ADVENTURE BEGINS

Unfortunately, Bella was in such a rush to get on with her journey, she didn't notice the large, menacing falcon.

"And so it begins," muttered the falcon as it circled high above the departing girl.

Like all animals, the falcon had the ability to see the merged outlines of Bella's human and nahual form at the same time. The fact that not all animals were quite as focused on doing this was down to their individual gifts of scrutiny and frame of mind at any particular time. For the falcon, it was the very thing he had been on lookout for. He could sense the power within her and compared it to the power of the ones she was soon to face.

"She has no idea," he squealed with glee. "It's as good as over." He let out a long, piercing squawk. Bella looked up quickly.

"Sounds like a war cry," she thought nervously. But the falcon had already swooped away.

When Bella first discovered her pendant and began flying as her animal twin, she'd had an overwhelming feeling of oneness with nature. It had reminded her of a time before the bullying started at school, when she had felt happy and free. These days, even her relationships with animals could sometimes be quite fractious – and not only with Prudence, the family cat. Crows, ravens – in fact, when Bella came to think of it, almost all black-winged birds as well as every bird of prey she came across – were becoming more aggressive towards her. If it wasn't for the fact that in her human form she held the upper hand, some of the more rebellious of these creatures might have already attacked. Keeping a watchful eye on the sky around her, Bella journeyed on.

It wasn't long before she found herself flying through the thick smoke bellowing out from various factories on the outskirts of London. Bella normally gave this part of the city a wide berth and had forgotten how bad the pollution was.

"And Britain is supposed to be leading the world in reducing greenhouse gases," she spluttered.

The Quetzal had made Bella feel guilty about her efforts to save the environment in her own day-to-day life. She considered how often she walked out of rooms leaving all the electrical appliances switched on.

"I need to put on a jumper sometimes," she reprimanded herself when she considered how often she'd ask her mum to crank up the central heating at the slightest hint of a chill. "And turn things off, rather than leaving them on standby all the time."

The air was much cooler and fresher once Bella made it to the sea. Subconsciously, perhaps, Bella might have hoped her flight was going to help her forget the unhappiness of the day. It wasn't long, however, until her mind returned to Charlie and Mickey.

"I hate him," she snarled through gritted teeth. "To think he actually kissed me!"

Even thinking about Mickey made her pendant turn

ice-cold. What worried Bella most was how she'd felt the pendant's warnings about Mickey, but still she failed to take any heed. "It was like there was something compelling me to do it," she admitted reluctantly.

"The power of your will is a remarkable force," scolded a voice inside her head. "For goodness sake, channel it in the right direction! Otherwise, we've no chance." Bella could sense how angry the spirit of Itzamna was and decided to keep her thoughts focused on navigation.

Thanks to directions given by a hundred different birds, Bella sustained a reasonably direct course, but it was a lonely, depressing journey. "There are so many car-jammed cities and factories messing up the air," she spat. "No wonder so many kids have asthma."

Somehow Bella soldiered on, fuelled by her deep yearning to be with her father. After a long, tiring night she found herself flying into a blazing sunrise towards the pyramids at Giza. Her first sight of the three sandstone landmarks, emerging with such a domineering presence over the city and the dusty terrain beyond, was spectacular.

"I'll have to stop," she told herself. "I need a rest anyway." Despite her tiredness, the gigantic structures reminded Bella of the wonder she'd felt at seeing the Temple of Tikal in Guatemala for the first time. There, the granite temples of the Maya towered up out of the rainforest like prehistoric skyscrapers, their deeply cut steps extending like colossal staircases into the heavens. Here, the lines of symmetry on the pyramids were much simpler and clearer to see because of openness of the site, extending high into the sky and the afterlife the ancient Egyptians believed awaited them there.

Bella came down to rest on the head of the mighty Sphinx herself and took in the breathtaking scene.

"I'm not surprised this place is one of the wonders of the world," she sighed. She gazed down at the large crowds of tourists queuing up to access the pyramids.

A small, plump-looking bird came down to perch alongside her. Bella admired the black-spotted pattern across his white feathers.

"How much further to Ethiopia?" she asked.

"Not another one!" chirped the bird, shaking the tuft of feathers sticking up from the crown of his head. "Seems like half the birds I meet are heading there this week – although I must say, you're the first parrot to ask."

"I'm not a parrot, I'm a quetzal!" Bella corrected him. "What are you?"

"I'm an Ethiopian spot-breasted lapwing," replied the bird proudly. "Visiting Egypt on a personal matter." Bella had no wish to pry into the lapwing's private life but the implication of his earlier remark made her curious.

"So, what kind of birds have you seen passing through?" she asked.

"Not the sort of multi-coloured birds like you would care for," replied the lapwing. "Vultures, eagles, falcons – it's the biggest migration of raptors anyone's ever seen." Bella recalled the harpy eagle who had so nearly killed the Quetzal at the Temple of Tikal last year. The thought of the sky being infested with such birds was alarming. "I should have waited for the Quetzal," she thought. "I might not be safe here on my own."

Just then, the sandstone beneath Bella's feet gave way. She slipped off the Sphinx's head but quickly managed to regain her balance and return to her spot.

"The whole thing's slowly falling apart thanks to human pollution," said the lapwing. "Give it a hundred years or so, there'll be nothing here but a pile of rubble."

Bella had no defence against the impact of her fellow humans on the planet, so she bid the lapwing farewell and journeyed on. Using the great River Nile as her guide, she headed south. She flew over the magnificent temples of Karnak and the rocky crevasses of the Valley of the Kings until she came to a wild, mountainous region. There, she looked down to see a scattering of buildings nestled into the lower slopes.

"Brrr," she shivered. Bella looked up to see that the warm sun on her back had been eclipsed by a blanket of dark-winged birds. Using the power of the pendant to magnify her view, she scrutinized the shadow. Suddenly, one solitary eagle dropping down ahead of the flock, opened her eyes to the horror heading straight for her.

"Raptors!" she cried.

The speed of their descent was unbelievable. Eagles, falcons, vultures – almost every species of preying birds imaginable – and all of them bearing the look of callous intent. She tried to manoeuvre herself out of their way, but there was no time.

"Aaaah!" she exclaimed as the thud of arched claws emptied her lungs. She felt her head and feet jerk violently forward as her body buckled. Spiralling downwards, she snatched glimpses of hundreds of sharply spiked beaks and talons ready, it seemed, to rip her to shreds.

"I love you, Mum," she shouted through the mêlée, grabbing the pendant and screwing her eyes tightly shut. "Charlie, I'm so sorry. I'm so, so sorry." Each breath was getting shorter and shorter.

"The power of your will is a remarkable force," urged her inner voice. "Hold on."

"I can't," she panted. "I can't . . ."

And then, darkness.

CHAPTER SIX

LALIBELA

Bella had sometimes wondered what the moment of her death would be like. She waited for her whole life to flash before her eyes but it didn't come. The reality was like some long, hideous nothingness filled with regret and an agonizing pain in her chest. Then, somewhere, way off in the distance, she heard a voice.

"Wake up and drink some coffee," it urged.

She opened her bleary eyes and found herself lying in a dimly lit room where a dark-skinned boy in his early teens was offering her a small, egg-shaped cup. "This will bring you strength," said the boy gently.

Bella's head was throbbing but she was at once entranced by the coffee's spicy aroma. It reminded her of the strange fragrances she'd come across in Diva Devaki's den in her Indian adventure last summer and for a moment wasn't sure if she should risk drinking it.

"Where am I?" she asked, taking the cup with a trembling hand.

"She speaks Amharic," someone gasped. Bella peered across the room to see a beautiful woman sitting cross-legged by a small charcoal fire.

"It's the girl," bleated the animal lying at her feet.

Bella rubbed her eyes. When she looked again she could see

that the goat appeared to have a resigned look on her face. Turning her attention to the woman, Bella wondered if she had recently been widowed, as she was dressed entirely in black. Then, jerked into the memory of her dramatic flight, Bella panicked.

"But how did . . .?" she started.

The boy rested a hand on her shoulder and for the first time Bella noticed the small red cross hanging from his neck on a thin leather cord.

"You're in a town called Lalibela in northern Ethiopia," he hushed. "I was out in the coffee fields yesterday lunchtime when you fell from the sky."

"Yesterday?" thought Bella. "Then I've been unconscious for hours." The thought was rather disturbing.

"One minute you were a bird, the next a girl," the boy continued. "I was there and you changed right before my eyes. Tell me – are you an angel?" Bella sensed a warm, mischievous glint in the boy's eye and liked him at once.

"I don't think my mum or my teachers would call me an angel," she replied with a blush.

Bella felt a little exposed that the boy had actually observed her transformation first-hand. "Well, whatever he thinks, he's being really helpful," she thought, taking a sip from her cup.

Ordinarily Bella hated the bitter taste of coffee, but she found this cupful was so smooth and sweet she drank the lot and at once began to feel refreshed. She also felt the power of the pendant tingling though her body and healing her wounds.

Bella watched as the woman threw incense onto the fire and poured coffee through the sweet-smelling smoke. She admired the boy's tall, proud stature and imagined he would make an excellent goalkeeper. Even in his sack-like rags, Bella could see there was a dignity about him that was striking.

"Who are you, then?" asked the boy with a smile. "You look like no other girl I've ever seen and yet you speak our language."

"My name's Bella – I'm Guatemalan, but I'm good at languages." The boy laughed.

"Did you jump from a plane?" he asked cheekily. Bella grimaced at the memory of her fall.

"Shhh, Yohanis," said the woman. "You're being rude. The poor girl's in pain."

Bella hesitated for a moment. It felt impossible to share the secret of her powers back home because everyone would think she was a freak.

"The quetzal bird you saw falling from the sky is my nahual," she told them cautiously. "I can transform myself into that form whenever I want to fly."

Bella was a little shocked at how easily she was able to share such a precious secret with someone she didn't even know. She examined Yohanis' face closely and was amazed by how accepting he looked.

"I think our special visitor could do with some more coffee, Mother," said Yohanis as he returned the cup.

"You must eat and rest, Bella," said Yohanis' mother kindly. "Can you sit up?"

Yohanis helped to prop Bella up against the wall while his mother reached for the charred-looking pots suspended above the fire. Bella's senses were sharpening. She noted that the mother also wore a small red cross around her neck – identical to the one worn by her son.

Bella cast her eyes around the room and saw that it was round and walled with wooden slats, packed with dry mud. The floor was made of mud too, uneven and hard, but nothing about it looked dirty. The only furniture Bella could see was the bed she was sitting on, which was made from logs held together with tightly-knotted rope. Apart from the rolled-up mats leaning against the walls and the neatly organized kitchen utensils around the fire, the only other feature of note was a beautiful painting of the Virgin Mary hanging on the wall above the bed.

"My name is Aster Alemnew," said the boy's mother kindly, passing Bella a round metal dish of food. Bella examined the brown, spongy circle and the large splodge of reddish paste. "Try this." Bella could smell the garlic.

"What is it?" she asked, and then realizing she might have sounded a little rude, added: "I've never had Ethiopian food before."

"It's called injera," Mrs Alemnew told her. "It's made from tef grain. The sauce is called wat."

Yohanis offered Bella a bowl of water and a towel to wash and dry her hands. Not entirely confident that she was doing the right thing, Bella ripped off a piece of injera, rolled it into a ball and dipped it into the sauce. To her relief, Bella found the food was delicious and her obvious appetite for the spicy sauce clearly pleased her hosts.

"Thanks," said Bella, slipping for a moment out of Amharic as she wiped the sauce from around her mouth. "Ameseginalehu. I didn't realize how hungry I was."

Bella felt so welcome and safe sitting here with these two strangers, it was as if she'd known them for years. "People can be so kind and generous," she thought. "I wish I had more time to stay here and get to know them better."

"Bella, I'm so sorry but Mother and I need to go to work this morning," Yohanis informed her while she ate. "I'll pop back in a few hours to see how you are. For now, you need to eat and relax. We'll talk tonight."

Bella was anxious to make her apologies and be on her way but Yohanis and his mother were already at the door.

"Goodbye, Bella," bleated the goat trotting after them. "I wish you all the strength you will need for the trials ahead."

The goat's farewell sounded a little disconcerting but Bella was so preoccupied with eating she didn't give it much thought.

"Rest a while," said a firm voice inside her head. "Replenish your energies."

"For a while, then," thought Bella, putting down the dish and lying back onto the bed. But there was too much on Bella's mind for her to sleep.

"What happened to me?" she wondered. "There was a whole army of raptors after me and yet I'm still alive."

"Luckily for you, they had other things on their mind," her inner voice told her. "They were so focused on where they were going they hardly noticed you were there. You were simply in their path."

As she lay in bed and allowed the power of the pendant to heal her injuries, Bella heard a distant pounding sound and idly wondered what it could be. She was actually beginning to doze off when she was startled by a piercing squeal from an animal in pain. "What was that?" she thought. She opened her eyes as a beam of sunshine burst into the room.

"Sorry, Bella," whispered a teenage girl as she closed the door behind her. "I forgot it was my turn to take breakfast to the priest." Bella sat up, shielding her eyes with her arm.

"Who are you?" she asked.

"My name's Mahlet," said the older girl. "I'm Yohanis' twin sister."

Bella was at once struck by the girl's beauty. Her long, dark hair was braided with coloured beads and her smile was so welcoming it put Bella at ease at once.

"You have a lovely home," said Bella. Mahlet laughed.

"And what about Yohanis?" she giggled. "Could he be a good-looking husband?" She gave Bella a playful wink and went over to the dwindling fire to collect the food and wrap it in a white cloth.

Like Yohanis, Mahlet wore a simple sackcloth robe and a highly visible red cross around her neck.

"Don't mind me," she told Bella, seeing the confused expression on Bella's face. "The girls round here are boy crazy. I'm only having a joke with you."

"My best friend Charlie is a bit like that at the moment," said Bella sadly. "We seem to have fallen out over a boy."

"It's not worth it," said Mahlet, coming over to the bed. "The way some people go on about it you would have thought nothing else in the world mattered."

Bella was often astounded on her adventures by how similar lives could be around the world.

"You must sleep," said Mahlet, turning to leave. "I'm sorry I disturbed you."

"No, wait," said Bella, quickly getting out of bed. "Thanks to Yohanis and your mother I'm feeling well enough to continue my journey."

In reality, Bella felt rather more wobbly on her feet than she'd expected.

"But you can't!" said Mahlet, offering Bella a steady hand. "We've arranged for the whole community to celebrate your arrival tonight with a feast."

"I'm really sorry," said Bella, brushing the dust from her clothes, "but I don't think I can stay." Bella couldn't help but feel embarrassed by her crumpled and shabby state.

"Mahlet looks so elegant," she thought. "And her clothes are so clean and pressed."

"I'm desperate to find my father," she told Mahlet.

"You're looking for your father too?" asked Mahlet. Bella thought she seemed a little vulnerable. "Then I understand."

Bella sensed that Mahlet wanted to say more, but she didn't press her new friend.

"Before you go, please come with me on my errand," Mahlet urged. "And then to the coffee fields to say farewell to Yohanis and my mother. They'll be upset with me if you don't." Bella nodded. It was the least she could do.

Mahlet led Bella outside. The dazzling morning sunshine was so hot, Bella started to sweat at once.

"What an amazing view," she gasped, gazing over the wild, mountainous terrain stretching out to the horizon. Despite the barrenness in the distance, the fields in the valley below were green and lush with clearly marked irrigation channels.

"It's been a good year for rain," said Mahlet. "The whole community has worked together to expand the coffee plantation our father set up. The harvest looks set to be the best we've ever had. Now, come on. There's an important maths test today and I need to get a good mark." Bella empathized at once.

"I hate maths tests," she replied sympathetically. "They're so boring."

Mahlet smiled. "That's probably because you find them easy," she said. "I spent the whole night revising. If I'm even going to get a chance of a university place in Addis Ababa, I need to come top of my class. Otherwise, I'll have to marry someone in Lalibela and work in the fields for the rest of my life." Bella felt a little uneasy and wasn't quite sure how to reply.

"Does Yohanis go to school?" she asked Mahlet.

"He gave up his place so that I could go," said Mahlet. "He spends all his time looking after the coffee plantation and running the cooperative as our father wished."

They were about to start walking when Bella noticed something that made her jump.

"What's that?" she asked, pointing to the furry black and white creature tethered to a nearby tree.

"That's our monkey, Guereza," said Mahlet, a little startled by Bella's outburst. "We've had him for four years now. He was orphaned and crippled by a hyena when he was a baby and we've been looking after him."

Bella noticed that the monkey's right foot was limp and turned inwards slightly. She felt sad to think that he was tied up.

"Do you keep animals?" asked Mahlet.

"My mum's got a cat," said Bella. "But we don't get on."

The monkey had a white beard that made him looked quite distinguished, but his down-turned face and drooping white tail appeared to tell its own story. As she looked him directly in the eye, Bella wondered if he had sensed her nahual. The fact that some creatures could see right through her, while others appeared oblivious, often struck Bella as odd. "But I suppose I don't always pay attention to what's happening around me," she thought.

On their walk through Lalibela, Bella noted that apart from a few two-storey buildings made from stone, most of the houses were round and made from wood and mud. Wherever they went there were women engaged in a whole range of activities. Some were washing clothes and hanging them out to dry over bushes, while others were stirring food in pots and maintaining fires, or pounding long poles into deep wooden mortars. Every one of them greeted Bella with a smile.

"Selam," they all said. "Selam," Bella replied.

A young pregnant mother, playing with her infant son in the shade of an acacia tree, invited them over for a coffee.

"I'm sorry," Mahlet told her. "We haven't any time right now." Bella might have felt happy to be here had it not been for what she saw next. It was the swarm of flies that alerted her.

"What's that?" she gasped, pointing to a carcass hanging by its hind legs from a nearby tree.

"We killed our goat in celebration of your arrival, Bella," said Mahlet cheerily, as an elderly woman with a knife began to cut away at the dead goat's hide. "We'd have gone out to hunt for rabbits or antelope but all the game seems to have disappeared."

Bella felt sick. "You killed that poor goat . . . just for me?" she stammered.

"But of course," said Mahlet. "You are our guest."

Bella felt too upset to speak. She ate meat and fish at home sometimes, but tried not to think of the poor animal that had actually died. Here, the connection was too close for comfort.

They walked on in silence for a while. Even in her trainers, Bella found the uneven path hard and uncomfortable and wondered how Mahlet could stand walking with bare feet. As a welcome breeze rattled the leaves and branches around her, Bella tried to turn her mind away from her sadness over the goat's fate.

"Where are all the men?" she asked Mahlet, realizing that apart from a few elderly men sitting in the shade, she'd seen hardly any grown men.

"Many, like my father, have gone off to fight in the war," said Mahlet. Bella could tell she was upset. "Those that are left tend to the cattle or hunt."

Bella wanted to ask Mahlet more about her father but decided to wait. She knew that war brought with it terrible things – she'd just never experienced any of them. Not yet.

As they walked on, it was perhaps because Bella was so full of sad thoughts that it took her a while to notice she was walking in the midst of an architectural wonder that surpassed anything she'd ever witnessed – even in Egypt or Guatemala. At one point, she could see three spectacular medieval temples, all of which were obscured to some degree by scaffolding.

"There's an ongoing programme of restoration," Mahlet told her. "Only sometimes, nothing is done for months."

"Who are those men?" asked Bella, observing the white-robed men who sat by cubicles carved into the rocks around the temples.

"They're priests," said Mahlet. "They're asking God for His blessing."

Bella was fascinated not only by the way the priests swayed gently forwards and backwards as they read from old leather-bound books, but by the sound of their ancient dialect. "It's like stepping right back into Biblical times," she thought.

"We have eleven rock-hewn churches," Mahlet told her as they stood before the most amazing church Bella had ever seen.

"You mean people actually carved this huge temple out of the rock with hammers and chisels?" she sighed in awe.

"With God's help," Mahlet replied. For a few moments Bella was lost for words.

Bella was enthralled by Lalibela. There was a peace and tranquillity here that was noticeably missing at the Temple of Tikal and the Egyptian pyramids because of the large number of tourists.

"This whole place feels like a unique, well-kept secret," she thought, feeling humbled by her opportunity to explore it. There was also the sense that despite her rush to get to her father, fate had brought her here for a reason.

"Your cross," remarked Bella, looking to Mahlet's neck. "Your brother and mother have one exactly like it."

Mahlet held the pendant between her fingers.

"It was a present from our father when he left for the war," she told Bella. "Something to remember him by."

Bella saw that Mahlet looked a bit sad.

"Come on, Bella," said Mahlet, walking a little faster. "I'm going to be late."

From some distance, Bella could see the tops of two towers peering up out of the ground.

"We're going to the Church of Saint George," said Mahlet. "You're going to love it!"

It wasn't until she arrived at the ridge of a massive chasm carved out of the rock that Bella realized what an incredible feat of architectural design stood before her. The towers of the church were massive, but hidden from view inside the human-made gorge.

"What an amazing church!" said Bella.

"Let me show you inside," said Mahlet proudly.

Bella's eyes drifted to a white-billed starling, tucked away inside a crack in the bell tower wall. The bird gave her a curious look.

They made their way down to the church along a winding passageway that eventually brought them out into the courtyard below. Bella followed Mahlet up the stone steps to the large, imposing doors.

"I have a cleaning job here in the afternoons after school," said Mahlet as she turned the round metal latch. "Everyone in Lalibela does what they can to take care of the churches and the poor."

As soon as she stepped inside, Bella felt the invigorating relief of the cool air.

"Phew!" she thought, running her fingers through her drenched, matted hair. "What a relief."

Bella quickly realized that she was stepping into a church of profound significance. Wooden torches cast a welcome, flickering light into the darkness, while all around her tapestries and paintings of incredible colour and beauty adorned the walls. "There are so many symbols here," she thought, recalling the markings on the walls of the Temple of Tikal. "Who knows what secrets they hold?"

Even in the dim torchlight, Bella recognized much of the

imagery in the paintings and tapestries from the stained-glass windows of churches she'd seen in London, but amongst these were battle scenes – some of them so bloody they made her wince. The centrepiece of the church was a rectangular turret with an elaborately carved door.

"You'll find every Orthodox Church in Ethiopia has one of these," said Mahlet. "They all hold a replica of the Ark."

Bella was busy exploring one of the tapestries, where eight black-armoured knights were engaged in a blood-thirsty battle. Unfortunately, the foot of the tapestry was charred and serrated. "It looks like it's been damaged by fire," thought Bella. "They should protect it with a glass frame or put it in a museum or something."

In the background of the tapestry were the imposing turrets and battlements of several medieval fortresses, and Bella tried to make out the image on the knight's shields behind the worn fibres.

"It looks like some kind of harpy," she thought, squinting her eyes as she imagined the half-women–half-vulture-like creatures of Greek mythology and the relentless way they harried their prey. "But something about these creatures here looks a little different."

The beasts on the knight's shields appeared to have the heads of armoured knights and the bodies of black, vulturine raptors. Bella withered at the sight of their sharp, clawed talons and long, scaly tails that extended down to a devilish spike.

"Did you hear what I said?" asked Mahlet, in an attempt to draw Bella's attention. "About the Ark."

"You mean the Ark of the Covenant?" Bella asked dubiously, turning her attention to the bolted door at the foot of the turret where Mahlet was standing. "The box Moses kept the Ten Commandments in?"

Bella really enjoyed all the films she'd seen and the stories she'd read about the Ark of the Covenant.

"Obviously it's just an old story, right?" Bella laughed.

Bella could tell by the look on Mahlet's face that as far as she was concerned, it was anything but.

CHAPTER SEVEN

TWO RAVENS

Mahlet left Bella to explore the artwork while she set off down a dark corridor to find the priest. It felt eerie to Bella, standing in a cold, dark church before such a violent picture. "I've seen some of these images before in that textbook Mickey was reading about the Knights Templar," she thought. "I wish I'd spent more time reading it."

Bella was searching the tapestry for clues as to what the Knights might have been fighting for when Mahlet returned.

"You say every church has a replica of the Ark," said Bella. "But what happened to the real one?"

"It's kept in a monastery in Axum up in the north of the country, surrounded by armed guards," Mahlet told her as they made their way out. "Everyone knows that."

Bella had the feeling that Mahlet was a little irritated with her. She was reminded also of that feeling she sometimes got at school when she put up a hand to ask a question that everyone else seemed to know the answer to.

As they stepped out into the mid-afternoon sunshine, Bella was again struck by the intensity of the heat.

"Is it always this hot?" she asked.

"It's supposed to be much cooler here in the highlands," Mahlet told her, her mood improving. "My mum says it's much hotter these days than it was when she was a child. Even in my lifetime, the land sometimes gets so dry that it's impossible to farm."

They were making their way towards the winding steps out of the chasm when they noticed a large golden eagle, circling high above them.

"There are so many birds of prey around here recently," said Mahlet. "It's no wonder all the local birds have gone."

Bella took the news badly. She had no doubt that it was a bad omen.

"But why?" she asked, walking briskly to keep up.

"It's as if these raptors are being drawn into the mountains by some powerful force," said Mahlet. Just then, Bella was struck by the sound of a distant whirring.

"Is that a helicopter?" she asked.

Mahlet nodded. "There's been a steady flow of them over the past few days, too," she told Bella. "We fear the war in the north is coming to a bloody climax. Many of the teenage boys have fled. They're scared another army recruitment convoy is going to drive through and force them to join the fighting. We've told Yohanis that he must hide in the mountains until the danger passes, but he refuses to go." Bella's pendant was turning cold.

"I don't know how I know this," she thought, "but this chill has nothing to do with the war Mahlet is referring to. It's to do with my father."

As soon as they made it back up onto the ridge above the church, Bella could see that indeed the sky was full of large birds of prey. It made her recoil with fear. "I need to lie low," she decided. "If any of these raptors see me flying as a quetzal, I'm dead." It was a depressing thought for a girl desperate to fly to her father's side.

Exhausted by their climb, Bella and Mahlet sat in the shade of a nearby eucalyptus tree.

"I'm already late for my maths test," said Mahlet with a sigh. "And we still haven't said goodbye to Yohanis and my mother. Oh, Bella, can't you stay tonight?" Bella suddenly reached out and put her hand across Mahlet's mouth.

"Shhh," she urged, quietly.

Bella was unnerved to hear the two large ravens perched high in the branches above. She'd never trusted black-winged birds, even as a young child. She had to strain, but Bella could just about make out what they were saying.

". . . I heard that we're to be called into battle any day now," one of them cawed. "Apparently the human girl our enemy has been waiting for is on her way. Everyone needs to be on the lookout for her. Her father waits for her somewhere further south, although no one seems to know for sure where he is. We'll get the full briefing from our leader up in the crater tonight."

Bella had to grab the pendant in her fist because it was so cold. "So it has got something to do with me and my father," she trembled. The thought that they were being spoken about in the context of a battle was deeply disturbing. She gazed into the sky, patrolled now by a dozen eagles in this area alone.

"You're listening to those birds," said Mahlet, aghast, when Bella removed her hand. Mahlet was staring at her with a look of intense curiosity.

"Shhh," Bella whispered, glancing up anxiously. Luckily the ravens were too engrossed in their conversation to notice them.

"Yohanis told me he saw you turn from a bird into a girl, but I thought he was joking," said Mahlet.

If she'd been back home talking with Charlie, Bella would have denied everything. "It's all true," she admitted, gesturing to her friend to keep her voice down. Mahlet looked shocked.

"There's no way I can fly to Lake Tana from here," thought Bella.

Bella knew that flying in the brightly coloured plumage of her nahual would be nothing less than suicide – she would be a target for every raptor in range. While many animals sensed her mystical powers at a glance even when she wasn't flying, they were much quicker to spot her when she took on her quetzal form. Bella tried to imagine what her father would do in her situation.

"I have to find out what's going on up in the mountains and report to my father before it's too late," she decided.

"Tell me," said Bella softly, turning to her bewildered friend, "is there a crater near here?"

"There's a dormant volcano high in the mountains," Mahlet nodded thoughtfully. "But there's nothing there."

"I'm going to have a look for myself," said Bella. "Tonight."

CHAPTER EIGHT

THE GUEREZA

Watching Mahlet run off to school, already late for her maths test, reminded Bella of her own life back home. "Sometimes you think life in other countries is going to be so different you'll never have anything in common," she mused. "But really, we're all getting on with the same things in life wherever we are." Bella felt a little guilty that Mahlet had worked so hard for a test only to risk getting zero because she'd been delayed. "It doesn't seem fair," she thought. But then, so many things about the world felt like that to Bella.

Feeling tired, Bella closed her eyes and drifted into a troubled sleep beneath the eucalyptus tree. She dreamt of a panicked Quetzal returning to 14 Birdcage Crescent back in London and finding her gone. She had a vision of her father, covered in blood and surrounded by ferocious beasts as he bellowed her name across a vast expanse of water. When she awoke, her heart was pounding and the late afternoon sun already had an orangey glow.

"Bella," someone was calling. "Bella, where are you?" It was Yohanis, stumbling up the track. "Mahlet said you might be here," he panted. "She said you wanted to visit the crater after dark. I've arranged to borrow three of our neighbour's donkeys – if that's alright?"

Bella's smile was all the reply Yohanis needed. She had no

intention of taking Yohanis and Mahlet with her on such a perilous journey, but knew they would only argue if she told them now.

"Thanks," she said, humbled as ever by the help of strangers in foreign lands.

"Come," said Yohanis. "I want to introduce you to my friends."

Yohanis led Bella back towards the town. Bella could tell by the low-lying sun in the west that she'd slept for most of the afternoon.

"How's the coffee harvest?" she asked.

"It's been the best we've ever had," Yohanis told her. "Even at the price the coffee company is offering, everyone in the cooperative will do quite well this year."

"Do you have a fair trade deal?" asked Bella.

Bella knew that such a deal would mean a guaranteed price for the coffee with a little extra to help plant more crops for the coming years.

"There's a big community meeting tomorrow night to discuss what we should do," Yohanis replied. "The man from the coffee corporation is offering goats to anyone who supports signing the cooperative over to their control."

"But that's bribery!" Bella cried. "What would your father think?"

Someone less intuitive than Bella might not have noticed the subtle droop in her friend's smile at her last remark. They walked on in silence until an old man in rags lying outside one of the churches asked Bella quite forcefully to give him some money.

"I'm sorry," said Bella, turning up the palms of her hands. "I don't have any."

"Go to hell," said the man with a dismissive toss of a hand. "You foreigners are all the same." Yohanis gave the man a glare and told Bella not to worry, but still she was ravaged with guilt.

"But I told him the truth," she told Yohanis.

"And tomorrow I too will tell the truth at this meeting with the community and the coffee company," said Yohanis. "But it won't do me any good."

They walked on a little further, and then Yohanis said, "I think my father must be dead."

"Why?" asked Bella, a little more loudly than she'd intended.

Yohanis stopped and turned to face her.

"Because six years is a long, long time to be away from the people you love – unless you are dead," he said. "And if he is still alive, then he obviously never loved us in the first place."

Bella understood the pain in Yohanis' voice.

"There were times when I felt like that about my own father," she told him, putting her hand on his shoulder. "But I was wrong."

Bella could see that her words had little effect on her friend's morale. "He's not only upset," she thought. "He feels angry and let down." Bella had empathy with these feelings too.

Yohanis' friends were gathered in a small dusty square in the middle of town, listening to a tiny radio. Bella could tell by their blue and white uniforms that they were on their way home from school.

"Don't you miss going to school with your friends?" she asked Yohanis.

"It's a luxury I can't afford," he replied sadly. "I'm head of the household now. Someone needs to work with my mother and bring in the money."

Around the square a few old men sat drinking coffee under the juniper trees. A young woman with a large pot wedged into a charcoal fire was clearly doing a roaring trade. Everyone seemed to be interested in what was being broadcast from the radio.

"What's happening?" asked Bella.

"They're listening to the World Athletic Championships," Yohanis told her. "We have three women in the ten-thousand-metre final."

Everyone in the square was on edge. Suddenly, there was an almighty cheer.

"Clean sweep!" Bella heard one of the boys shout. "Gold, silver and bronze!" The atmosphere was electric. It reminded Bella of being in the crowd at a football match whenever Charlton scored.

"We have the best long-distance runners in the world," said Yohanis proudly.

To Bella's delight, she saw that one of the boys had a ball made from plastic bags and elastic bands – almost identical to the ones she'd seen in Guatemala and India.

"We play here every afternoon," Yohanis told her.

"Let's have a game," said Bella, before Yohanis even had a chance to introduce her.

"Girls don't play football," laughed Yohanis, looking amazed.

"If we can win gold, silver and bronze in the ten-thousand-metre, we can play football," Bella pointed out. "Which is the quickest way back to your house?"

Within twenty minutes Bella had found Mahlet as well as three other girls they managed to persuade en route. Against a barrage of complaints from the boys as well as a few from disgruntled onlookers, the girls all joined in on two hastily chosen teams.

"Go for it, girls!" rooted the woman with the large coffee pot. "You show them."

To start with, the boys were reluctant to pass to the girls, but that didn't last for long and soon everyone was getting stuck in.

"That was great fun," Mahlet puffed when it was all over.

"And you were all really good," cheered Yohanis. "You girls should come down here more often."

"Perhaps if my brother helped out in the kitchen a little more, I could," said one of the other girls, giving another boy a measured look.

On the way back to her friends' house, Bella passed a happy gathering of people doting on a baby in a shawl.

"Remember that kind lady who invited us over for coffee this morning?" said Mahlet. "Well, that's her newborn baby."

While Yohanis went on ahead to help his mother, Bella and Mahlet were delighted to hold the beautiful baby girl.

"She looks so warm and cozy inside this shawl," Bella smiled. "And how's her mother?"

"She's resting," said Mahlet. "In our culture, the community takes care of all the housework until she feels strong again."

By the time they got back, the evening festivities were about to begin. Although Bella was anxious to get to her father, she was at least relieved that her plans to visit the crater gave her a little more time to spend with her friends. "Don't worry, Father," she whispered into the wind. "I am coming."

"Sorry, Bella," said Mahlet. "I didn't quite hear you."

"Erm . . . I can smell fresh coffee," said Bella quickly, feeling a little embarrassed.

Even in the dim light cast by a dozen sparkling lanterns, Bella could see the many pots of coffee bubbling away on small charcoal fires all around her.

"Would you like some?" asked Mahlet. "It will help to keep you awake for the long journey tonight."

"I think I'd better," said Bella. "But first I'd like a big glass of water, if that's okay. Football is thirsty work."

While Mahlet was away, Bella watched Mrs Alemnew, along with a team of twenty or so other women, serving injera and ladles of spicy meat and vegetable sauces from large pots. Laying them out on big, flat dishes, they distributed the food to groups of four or five people who would then all share from the same plate. Bella was touched by the way whole families were eating together.

"You're all so welcoming," Bella told Yohanis when he arrived back with a big dish of food.

"We don't get many visitors," he replied as they sat down at a small charcoal fire away from the main gathering. "And when we do, they rarely fall out of the sky." He gave Bella a playful grin that filled her with a sense of understanding and friendship.

A small band of musicians sitting right at the centre of the festivities began to play their flutes and goat-skin drums. The dulcet strains of their warbling melodies calmed even the distant cries of the newborn baby.

"I love this music," said Bella, taking her water and coffee from Mahlet when she returned. "It's so peaceful."

"I prefer the songs you can dance to," said Yohanis, passing Bella a small bowl of water in which to wash her hands.

It wasn't long before they were all tucking into their food. While the conversation between them lulled, Bella began to listen to the people chatting around her. Even without using her powers, she could hear some of the villagers talking about tomorrow night's meeting with the coffee company.

"Don't listen to them," she heard Mahlet whisper to Yohanis. But raised voices from a nearby fire were turning nasty.

"Of course we should sell to the coffee company!" yelled an old man, directing his stick at a small group of fellow elders. "Yohanis can't be expected to handle the business without his father. He has neither his father's vision nor his skill."

Yohanis jumped to his feet.

"Stay calm," Mahlet hushed. "Treat the elder with disrespect at your peril."

Clearly enraged by the comments, Yohanis clenched his fists and walked away.

"Why doesn't he say something?" Bella urged Mahlet, angrily.

"Because he knows he must control his anger and focus on what he needs to do," she replied. Bella felt a twinge of embarrassment.

"I must learn to control my anger, too," she thought, acknowledging how often her rash feelings got her into trouble.

It was then that Bella noticed a tall, blond-haired man in a blue suit, slipping away with his briefcase. He'd obviously been lurking in the shadows because his European appearance was too out-of-place to miss in the open.

"Who's that?" she asked.

"That's Mr Letellier from the coffee company," replied Mahlet. "He arrived by helicopter earlier this morning. He'll be speaking at the meeting tomorrow night."

"So what's he doing hanging around here now?" Bella hushed.

"Lobbying for support, I guess," said Mahlet.

Bella had a bitter taste in her mouth. "There are sinister dealings going on here to make money out of these honest, hard-working people," she thought, getting up to go and speak her mind to Mr Letellier.

"Please don't." A hand grabbed her arm. She turned around to find Yohanis, his face etched with anxiety.

"I know what you're thinking," he told her. Bella was shocked by the firmness of his tone. "If you stand up to him in front of the entire community, others will argue that I'm taking on your views – the opinions of a foreigner who can't possibly know what's right for us." Bella felt ashamed. "Focus on your own journey," he urged her. "I'll deal with the man from the coffee company."

He left Bella and Mahlet and went to help his mother dish out food to some of the local beggars, including the one who'd been so unfriendly towards Bella earlier. Bella sat back down by the fire. As she followed Yohanis' departure, Bella noticed that the Guereza was now hobbling freely around the party, picking up quite a feast. When Mahlet got up to go and find her brother, the monkey limped across and crouched by Bella's side.

"Be careful who you trust," he told her, reaching out to grab a big piece of injera from Bella's plate. Bella was taken aback by his abruptness. "I heard a story once," the Guereza continued. "It was about a human girl with exceptional powers." Bella felt uneasy. "The story foretold that with the animals of the world behind her, the girl would lead them in a great battle, the outcome of which would become destiny itself and the start of all mythologies to come." Bella stopped eating and put down her plate.

"But it's only a story, right?" she asked hopefully. "There isn't really going to be a great battle." Bella's monkey voice immediately aroused interest from two children nearby. The Guereza climbed into Bella's lap and looked her straight in the eye.

"The wheels are already in motion," he grinned. "And it's not only the birds who are out to get you."

CHAPTER NINE

THE BLACK-HEADED JACKAL

The festivities in Lalibela were in full swing as Yohanis and Mahlet led Bella to the outskirts of town and the three donkeys Yohanis had tethered to a wild olive tree.

"Before we go any further," Bella started nervously, "I need you to understand that this is a journey I must make on my own." The children looked devastated.

"But you don't know what dangers the mountains hold," Mahlet argued.

"Or the best path to take," Yohanis added.

For a moment Bella didn't know what to say. Their company alone was something she was going to miss very much, but she knew she was right.

"Tomorrow's meeting with the coffee company is a challenge that you must face alone," she told Yohanis. "For your father and for the future of your family." Yohanis nodded thoughtfully. "And so this is for me," said Bella. "This is my journey."

No amount of arguing from her Ethiopian friends could shake Bella's resolve. And so, with heavy hearts, Yohanis and Mahlet untied the largest of the donkeys and led Bella to the start of the mountain path.

"Follow this trail through the coffee fields and on to the springs," said Mahlet as they helped Bella up into the saddle.

"Then at each junction take the steepest ascent." The donkey snorted.

"Eventually you will come to a cave where the Balai lives," said Yohanis. "He's the old man our community pays to tend to our goats. Sometimes he shepherds them on the upper slopes close to the crater's edge."

"Give him this," said Mahlet, passing Bella a healthy supply of injera wrapped in a cloth. "And here, this is for you." She handed Bella a beautifully pressed sackcloth shawl. "It gets really cold in the mountains at night." Bella gratefully accepted this gift. The temperature had fallen quite dramatically since they'd left the warmth of the fires.

"With a little rest, the donkey will be strong enough to bring you straight back down again in the morning," said Mahlet.

"Just in time for work," grumbled the donkey. But Bella couldn't think beyond finding out what was going on at the crater and tracking down her father.

Yohanis gave the donkey a friendly tap on the back and Bella was off.

Even on relatively flat ground, Bella found the jerks and jolts of the donkey's stride uncomfortable and instantly tightened her grip.

"Ouch!" complained the donkey. "You're bruising me." Bella tried to relax her hold but it wasn't easy.

With a crisp breeze in her face and the smell of ripening coffee beans all around her, they were almost out of the plantation when a loud, uneven thud alerted Bella to a surprise companion.

"Wait for me!" shrieked the Guereza, limping up and flinging himself up onto the donkey's back.

"Planning on giving anyone else a lift?" grunted the donkey.

The Guereza wrapped his long hairy legs tightly around Bella's body.

"Watch out for the jackals," he warned them. "They're worse than the snakes."

The sound of a human speaking to a monkey awoke the mosquitoes to Bella's presence and there was soon a swarm of them buzzing around her head.

"You'd better not bite," Bella warned them. The Guereza clapped his hands above his head to send them on their way.

"We must speak in hushed tones," he told her. "Treachery is everywhere."

The Guereza's words filled Bella with dread. "What am I getting myself into?" she wondered.

Even after an hour's climb, the driving beat of the drums from Lalibela could still be heard. Bella looked down upon the distant fires and wondered how long it would be before she would be amongst friends again.

It was the Guereza who first noticed the tiny black dot that was circling high above them.

"Looks like a golden eagle," he observed. "He's probably acting as a marker for any late arrivals."

"What do you mean?" asked Bella, a little startled. "You talk as if you know what's happening."

"I hear things," said the Guereza warily.

Bella tried to press the Guereza further but he wasn't to be drawn. All her questions succeeded in doing was to make them all feel tense.

Bella wrapped Mahlet's shawl a little tighter around her body. "I didn't think anywhere in Africa would feel this cold," she shivered to herself.

They travelled on in silence until they reached the springs. There they stopped for a drink before taking the steep path leading into the mountains. "Poor donkey," thought Bella, as he hauled himself on. "I don't know how he does it."

Startled by a loud rustling sound, Bella looked up to see an antelope peering over a wiry fruit bush.

"Who goes there?" it snorted.

The donkey stopped. Bella sensed from the antelope's kind face and delicately pointed ears that she had a gentle nature.

"It's a mountain nyala," the Guereza whispered.

"She looks a little scared," said Bella.

"So the rumours are true," said the Nyala, less jittery now that they were talking. She trotted around the bush to examine Bella at close hand. Bella admired the white stripes on the Nyala's brown shaggy coat before noticing her scar.

"What happened to your neck?" asked Bella.

The Nyala shook her head with disgust.

"Attempted murder," she told them. "For the last few days foreigners with rifles have been rampaging through the mountains killing everything in sight. Someone, somewhere, is having quite a party."

"What do you know about the girl?" asked the Guereza through chattering teeth.

Bella felt disconcerted and cross. "They're talking about me as if I'm not even here," she thought.

"They say that she's needed for the battles ahead," the Nyala replied, becoming more spirited. "Only we didn't believe she actually existed."

"Well, she does!" said the Guereza, glancing around nervously.

"I can see that now," said the Nyala. "The question is, can she do anything to help? Tonight our enemies are assembling the largest animal army ever known. They will attack the girl's father and every living creature who stands alongside him." Bella was horrified.

"What kind of enemy are we up against?" she wondered. Bella felt as cold as her pendant. "I need to see what's going on in the crater," she announced decisively. "Can you help?"

The Nyala probed Bella's eyes for the fiery spirit alluded to in the old stories. The girl was said to have inner powers matched only by those of her legendary father.

"The best thing I can do is send word to our allies," the Nyala told her. "If tonight's mission is successful, you'll need help to reach your father quickly." The thought of some support was uplifting to Bella. "Get caught, and our cause is lost," the Nyala concluded. And with that she turned and galloped away into the night.

"Can we get on with the climb now?" groaned the donkey. Bella clicked her heels and gave him a grateful pat on the neck.

They journeyed on for half an hour before anyone spoke.

"I'm bushed," grunted the donkey. "What happened to dinner?"

"Ignore him," said the Guereza. "Donkeys are always hungry and fed up – doesn't matter how much food you give them." Still, Bella felt bad to be getting an easy ride at the donkey's expense and resolved to do everything she could to repay him.

Several times on the journey, Bella thought she saw shimmerings in the dust. Scared of an ambush, she reached for her pendant and rubbed it between her fingers for reassurance.

"I'm catching a cold," the Guereza wheezed, his condensing breath clearly visible now. "Monkeys shouldn't hang around in places too high for trees."

It took them the best part of three hours before a break in the cloud allowed the moon to illuminate the summit.

"Ever climbed over volcanic rock before?" asked the Guereza sceptically, as they gazed up at the sheer face. Bella shook her head. "I hear it can rip through clothing and into your skin."

Bella observed how the colour of the rock became more ashen as the gentle slopes veered up towards the final ascent into the mist. It was a daunting moment but there was no turning back now. She scoured the slopes and found that where the ashen rock gave way to a much darker terrain further down the mountain, there was a small, glittering fire. Using the power of the pendant to magnify her vision, Bella saw a solitary figure surrounded by tiny white specks.

"I can see the Balai and his goats," she said. "We're nearly there."

They continued with new vigour but their route was so scattered with sharp turns and steep climbs it was slow going. To compound things further, there were huge fractures in the rock that made it difficult for the donkey to keep his footing.

When they finally made it to the Balai's cave, his slight, stick-like figure looked so fragile and brittle, Bella wondered how he could possibly survive in such a remote place.

"Not much meat on him, is there?" said the Guereza. "No wonder the jackals don't bother him."

"But why does he spend his nights here?" asked Bella. "There's hardly anything for the goats to eat."

"Fewer predators to worry the goats," replied the Guereza. "It's too high for jackals. They'd sooner hunt for bushbuck and gazelle further down the mountain. As soon as the Balai senses trouble he takes the goats into his cave and lights a fire."

Bella gave the old hermit the gift of food from Mahlet and told him her plan to see inside the crater. With every word Bella spoke, the crags in his weathered forehead deepened. By the end of her story, his face was so etched with displeasure, it was unnerving.

"Take the goats," he croaked. "With any luck, they'll think you're herders." He stamped out his fire and retired into his cave. Bella wasn't sure what she should have expected but still felt a little rejected by the Balai's abruptness.

"He didn't say very much," she whispered to the Guereza.

"He's a hermit," replied the monkey. "What do you expect?"

Bella and the Guereza left the donkey to rest, gathered a small herd of goats and started to make their way towards the summit. A few minutes into their trek, a speeding helicopter tracked by a flock of fearsome-looking birds swooped right over them. Guereza, clearly terrified for his life, clamped himself around Bella's body and hid under her shawl.

"Where did they come from?" Bella exclaimed. They watched the helicopter and birds disappear into the crater.

Suddenly a long, haunting howl ripped through the night. Using her powers, Bella saw the silhouette of a large canine beast standing on a rocky outcrop a mile or so to the east. Its sharp pointed ears and stiffened posture left Bella in little doubt that it was on the hunt.

"Sounds like a black-headed jackal," the Guereza

trembled. "And it's not only the goats he'll be after if he catches our scent!"

"Get back to the Balai's cave as quickly as you can," Bella ordered the goats. The animals speedily obliged.

"Shan't be sorry to see the back of her," she heard one of them bleat through the clank of bells.

"She's the girl from the stories," she heard another reply.

"I don't care," came the retort. "She's too bossy and too small." Bella strained her ears to catch their fading voices. "That jackal's in for an easy lunch, you mark my words."

Gathering her powers, Bella began to scramble up towards the summit.

"You have the strength of a baboon," the Guereza puffed, doing his best to keep up. But Bella was in no mood to talk. The volcanic rock tore her clothes and drew blood from her knees and hands but still Bella gritted her teeth and forced herself on. Clambering up onto the ridge of the crater, she peered warily down.

The second Bella's head cleared the ridge she was hit by a wall of sound – as if someone had just opened the door upon the biggest aviary in the world and let in the cats. To her horror, every nook and crevice of the crater's gigantic interior was occupied by raptors. Every species, size and type Bella could imagine was there, from huge eagles, vultures and larger hawks, right down to the smaller species of falcons. But that wasn't all. Speckled about the crater, a motley array of crows, rooks and ravens were asserting themselves with a never-ending cacophony of caws. "I might have guessed this lot were all embroiled with the enemy," thought Bella.

The natural architecture of the crater reminded Bella of

those massive gladiatorial auditoriums she'd seen in films. Only here, instead of a fight as a spectacle, there were seven awesomely armed military helicopters and a small parade of human militia. Dressed in black with metallic shields, helmets and visors, the militia carried rifles, giving them the air of modern-day knights.

"Are you alright?" the Guereza whispered. "You look like you're going to be sick."

"What's that rancid smell?" Bella asked, pulling her shawl over her nose.

She almost gagged when he pointed out the hundreds of animal carcasses impaled on long poles all around the crater.

"Someone's feeding this army up," said the Guereza, "building their strength for battle."

"Regiments to your positions." The order came from a magnificent steppe eagle perched beneath the crater's lip. Bella admired the large, brown-bodied bird as it fully extended its wings and dropped from its perch. Following the eagle's command, there were swift, well-organized manoeuvres, both on the terraces and in the crater itself, where the soldiers were assembling as if in preparation for an imminent inspection. Bella's pendant was so cold now it hurt.

"Two minutes," came the announcement over a loudspeaker.

At the centre of the crater was a small platform upon which a podium had been erected. Before it, a large ornate cloth was covering something, giving it the appearance of a table. Following the announcement, seven men in dark business suits climbed down from one of the helicopters and took up positions on the podium.

"This is weird a place for businessmen," thought Bella.

"What's going on here?"

The loose stones around Bella and the Guereza's feet began to give way as the down thrust of a huge military helicopter caked them in dust. Armed to the hilt with rockets and machine guns, the helicopter descended into the crater.

"That was close!" the Guereza spluttered, pulling himself up a little higher.

"Get down and keep still," said Bella, yanking him down.

They watched the helicopter land on the crater floor. Humans and raptors alike stood to attention as twenty more soldiers jumped out and formed a protective passageway to the platform.

"They're preparing to meet their leader," thought Bella.

And then he appeared. Even from a great distance, Bella could see that the figure disembarking from the craft had an aura that commanded respect. Not only was he strikingly tall, he was broad-shouldered and looked incredibly strong. Refusing to duck his head for the propellers rotating only centimetres above his head, the man marched down the line of saluting soldiers. Using the power of her pendant, Bella focused her powers and magnified his form. She watched him carefully take off his long, black overcoat to reveal a sharp, dark-blue suit, silky-blue shirt and tie. He would have looked the very image of business conformity had it not been for his long, jet-black hair and thick facial stubble. He'd almost made it to the platform when Bella noticed the blond-haired man about to hand him the microphone.

"That's Mr Letellier from the coffee company," she gasped.

"Comrades," Letellier announced. "Noble members of the Corporation board. It is my humble honour to introduce General Karpov."

A roar of excitement erupted as birds everywhere opened their beaks and throats to squall with delight.

"I've heard about this Corporation in the news," Bella realized. "They were in New York lobbying world leaders only a few days ago."

Bella and the Guereza stared goggle-eyed as Karpov took the platform and inspected those before him.

"It's time," he began, his voice booming out through the speakers so loudly it caused feedback.

"Ow!" cried the Guereza, clamping his hands over his ears. "That hurt."

"Shhh!" Bella warned him, pushing his face down into the dirt.

"He sounds American," thought Bella, a little surprised; she'd expected Karpov's accent to be Russian.

Karpov's expression was thunderous. He took a step back while one of his minions dabbled with the microphone. Dismissing the technician with an irritated flick of his wrist, Karpov stepped forward.

"Our enemy's forces are gathering," he continued. "They're awaiting the arrival of the human girl from the ancient prophesies in the hope of resurrecting their miserably lost cause." Bella was numb with fear. "Even as I speak, our intelligence forces are hunting both the girl and the man they call the Baläm. I want to know everything that passes between them. The secret of their mystical powers would do much to strengthen us even further."

Bella knew at once that this Baläm was her father. Baläm was the name the K'iche' tribe gave to the jaguar, the most revered beast, not only in Guatemalan mythology, but throughout the rainforests – even today.

"Well he won't get many secrets from me," thought Bella, who imagined she had as many questions for her father as Karpov did.

"Then, once we have them both firmly in our sights," Karpov continued, "we'll move in for the kill. With the girl and her father out of the equation, we'll simply wipe their army right off the face of the earth."

Karpov stopped and turned to the elaborate fabric before him. He gathered the cloth up in his hands ready to swish it away. The crowd tensed with expectation. It was at that precise moment that the Guereza sneezed.

CHAPTER TEN

ON THE RUN

The Guereza's untimely sneeze had the effect of a flare rocketing up into the pitch-black sky. Karpov released his grip of the cloth and quickly looked up.

"You idiot!" grimaced Bella, throwing herself face down onto the hard volcanic rock. But it was too late. With a deafening yowl and a cascade of falling rocks, the Guereza was tumbling down the mountainside.

"Watch out!" someone shouted. But the vicious claws of the black-headed jackal were already upon her.

"Ahhh!" Bella screamed as the jackal's claws slashed down her right arm. She tried to roll away but the beast was all over her, lashing at her face with his razor-sharp claws. "Get off me!" she bawled, pushing at his underbelly and turning her head into the dirt. Quite by chance the jackal caught the chain of her pendant and ripped it from her neck.

"No!" she hollered, yanking herself up.

"Keep your head down!" Bella had no idea who the voice belonged to and things were happening far too fast to look. She heard the swift rush of air as something shot past her right ear.

"What was that?" she thought as she flinched and turned away.

Thud! There was an agonizing howl from the jackal. Bella looked up to see a spear hanging from the jackal's hind leg, blood spurting from the wound.

"Run!"

She glanced down to see the Balai as he aimed a second spear at the jackal.

"But my pendant!" thought Bella. The jackal was tottering right over it, his eyes willing her to come and get it.

"Head back to the cave!" called the herdsman as he lurched forward to grab Bella's arm. His spear had penetrated the jackal's back leg but still the beast pursued them. They scurried down the slope, throwing up a cloud of dust in their wake. Above them, the ear-splitting cries of the eagles were quickly followed by their first vicious offensive. Pecking and snapping violently at their heads, one of eagles clamped on to Bella's ear.

"Off!" she yelled, whacking it away with the back of her bleeding hand. Their clothes and hands lacerated by the sharp rocks and prickly scrub, Bella and the herdsman made it to the gentler slopes and began to sprint.

"Where's the monkey?" Bella called, looking back. But there was no sign of him anywhere. To their fleeting relief, they could see that the jackal's injury had forced him to abort his attack. With a flock of birds harrying them all the way, Bella and the Balai reached the cave where a big fire was already blazing. Repelled by the flames, the birds scattered, circling the fire and guarding every escape route.

"We need to be swift," snorted the beast who stepped out of the shadows.

"Nyala!" exclaimed Bella. "But what are you . . ."

"Quickly!" the Nyala ordered. "Jump onto my back."

The Balai hoisted Bella up onto the Nyala's back.

"Thank you," Bella told the Balai. "And please, could you make sure the donkey gets back safely?" The Balai nodded as he gave the Nyala a slap on the back.

"Now, go!" he told them.

"Wrap your hands around my neck," the Nyala urged as she galloped away.

Bella was astounded by the antelope's courage. Armed with nothing but the crown of her head, she butted away any raptor in her path and sped off down the mountain.

With the cold wind racing through her hair, Bella looked up into the sky, alive with dark-winged creatures in hungry pursuit.

"Where are we going?" she asked, sensing that the Nyala had made a tactical turn towards the south.

"We need to get undercover," the Nyala puffed. "We're too exposed this high in the mountains."

Down, down, down they fled, the Nyala taking great leaps over boulders and landing with incredible precision on the rocky terrain beyond.

"But how did you know . . .?" Bella began.

"I heard the jackal," replied the Nyala. "Now stop talking and hold on."

The further down the mountain they raced, the more trees and shrubs there were until, in the distance, Bella could make out the shape of a much denser canopy. Bella looked over her shoulder as the eagles moved in. They were tracking them so closely now that Bella could actually hear the steppe eagle giving his commands.

"Bring down the nyala," he ordered. "Then peck out her eyes." Immediately two enormous eagles broke away from the main formation and flanked the Nyala's head.

"Hold on!" shouted the Nyala in desperation.

Bella swiped out at the eagle to her left, catching his wing and sending him spiralling out of control into the bushes. The second eagle lurched for the Nyala's eye with its beak and caught the full impact of Bella's fist. But just as Bella thought they were making headway against the barrage from the air, the ground forces attacked.

"Dogs!" the Nyala cried in terror.

Suddenly, as if out of nowhere, ferocious wild dogs were snapping around the Nyala's delicate feet. Against a cacophony of hostile barks and gnashing jaws, two dogs launched themselves up and dug their sharp teeth into the Nyala's hind legs. Her knees buckled and Bella was jettisoned over the antelope's head.

CHAPTER ELEVEN

THE MIGHTY KUDU

"No!" Bella screamed, as two wild dogs jumped onto her chest and pinned her down to the ground. Hot clouds of dank breath poured from their snouts as globules of warm, frothy saliva splattered over Bella's face.

"Argh!" Bella growled, thrashing out with her fists as she tried to gather her mystical powers without the pendant. There was a painful yelp, followed by the sound of hysterical barking and the two dogs standing on Bella leapt away. Bella caught the look of horror in their eyes and turned around. To her astonishment, a stupendous, grey-coated antelope with magnificent spiralling horns – at least a metre and a half long – was glaring down at the pack. Bella sensed several of the dogs flinch, but none retreated.

"They're up for a fight," Bella shuddered.

The Nyala tried to jerk herself up onto her feet, but collapsed in the blood-stained dirt.

"Nyala – are you alright?" Bella spluttered, but there was no reply.

The dogs were agitated, turning in small circles and clawing in the air.

"Give us the girl and we'll back off," snarled the largest dog, gnashing his teeth. "This isn't a scrap an old kudu like you can win. Not against the pack."

Bella was impressed with how regally the mighty kudu stood his ground and lowered his horns. Several of the smaller dogs shuffled back.

"You're making a mistake," warned the big dog.

Bella felt her anger stir. She hated the smugness of the dog's tone. It reminded her of the way human bullies at home hung around in gangs and tossed insults at their victims.

"I'm not the one making the mistake," snorted the Kudu. "You are. They said the girl would never come. Well, she has."

The malicious growl of the pack's leader roused a chorus of aggravated yelps. Bella felt her body stiffen. Then, in an explosion of synchronized aggression, the dogs attacked.

Bella scrambled away, terrified by the ferocity of their onslaught. But the Kudu was ready for them. Bella watched in amazement as he swept away two of the dogs with his horns, before kicking away another with his hind legs.

"He's awesome," gasped Bella. "But there are too many of them!"

She grabbed the thickest fallen branch she could find and charged into the pack. Swinging the branch around her body with such speed that none of the dogs could get near her, Bella and the Kudu counterattacked.

"Leave them," yapped the pack leader, his resolve punctured by the sharp swipe of the Kudu's mighty horns. The dogs stood down and began backing off. "Let them have this puny little victory," snarled the leader, turning to leave. "The girl will never get past the mountain wolves."

As the dogs scampered away, Bella dropped her weapon and staggered over to join the Kudu as he stood over the Nyala's limp, bloodstained body.

"Is she alright?" Bella panted. The Kudu was nuzzling the Nyala's snout. Bella knew by the tears in his eyes that the news was bleak.

"She'd dead," the Kudu replied at last. "I was too late."

Bella fell to her knees, engulfed by a wave of exhaustion and grief and laid her head against the Nyala's cheek.

"You saved my life," she sobbed, wiping the tears from her own eyes.

The Nyala, the gentle antelope, had defended her against these brutal aggressors with no regard for her own safety.

"She did her duty," replied the Kudu respectfully. "And for that, we must all draw inspiration and courage in this time of need."

High above, the screeches of a hundred raptors reminded every creature in earshot how turbulent these times were.

"Onto my back," said the Kudu. "We'll find shelter in the woods."

And so, for the second time within the hour, Bella was whisked away from raptors by an antelope loyal to her father's cause.

As the Kudu galloped into the forest, the sound of raptors gradually faded into the distance.

"How come you were there to rescue me?" called Bella, wondering how much influence her father and their cause could wield in the animal world.

"I had a visit from a white-billed starling yesterday morning," the Kudu panted. "She sent word about your unexpected arrival."

"I was blasted out of the sky," Bella complained, recalling the starling she'd seen at the Church of Saint George. The little bird had been tucked away inside a crack in the wall a few metres below the bell tower.

"What you have to understand, my friend," the Kudu told her, "is that up until now, you've been nothing but a rumour." He broke from a run into a quick canter. "Now you're here, you should find that you have almost as many allies as you do enemies in the animal world."

"But how am I to know which ones are on the lookout to help me and which ones will betray me?" Bella asked, exasperated. It took a moment for the Kudu to consider his response.

"That's a hard one to answer," he replied, as he leapt over the trunk of a fallen tree. "While it might seem obvious to some humans that all raptors, snakes and crocodiles are more open to evil than creatures such as doves, rabbits and antelopes, it would be a big mistake to make such an assumption a statement of fact."

Bella well understood the idea of never judging anyone by their appearance alone. All the same, she was going to find it hard to have a positive attitude towards jackals and wild dogs for quite some time.

"So it's simply down to individual animals making their own choices between good and evil?" she queried.

"Something like that," the Kudu replied. "And even that can change over time. As to which animals can see you for who you are – well that's simply down to how closely they look. Most animals are too busy getting on with their lives to even notice you."

Nothing the Kudu was saying brought Bella comfort.

"Then where are all the other animals like you?" she asked, a touch irritated.

"We're around," replied the Kudu. "We've just been a little slow to join your father's campaign."

"You know my father?" asked Bella excitedly.

"Not personally," said the Kudu. "Only by reputation. He's organizing a big summit meeting by the shores of Lake Tana."

"I know," Bella interjected. "That's where I'm going." The Kudu nodded.

"Many animals from these parts have gone to meet your father there," the Kudu told her, "but most have stayed behind. It's not that they don't support his cause, you understand. It's because they feel too powerless to make any difference."

Bella understood. Many of her mum's friends back home admired her support for various charities and marches but would never dream of getting involved themselves. The Kudu slowed to a trot.

"We're safe here in the woods," he reassured her. "There may be the odd earthbound creature who bears an allegiance to your father's enemies, but they won't harm you here." Bella felt relieved to hear this, although she half suspected the reasons for her safety had more to do with the comment made by the wild dog about leaving her to the wolves. "They're biding their time," she thought.

Bella thought back to the events up at the crater. She was worried about the fate of the Guereza. "What if he was killed by the fall?" she thought. "And what if he was injured and the raptors got to him? The poor thing would have been pecked to death!" The thought filled Bella with fear for her newfound friend. As for the kind herdsman who'd saved her from the black-headed jackal, Bella had nothing but heartfelt regard.

"Without him, I would have perished for sure," she told herself.

The sweet smell of eucalyptus trees and the crisp crunch of the undergrowth brought Bella comfort and reminded her of the woods close to her home in London. They journeyed on for almost an hour, zigzagging through the undergrowth to the welcoming chirps of the birds in the lower canopies. Since discovering she had a quetzal as her nahual, Bella had become quite an expert on exotic birds.

"There's an Arabian bustard and a spot-breasted lapwing," she cheered. "And if I'm not mistaken, I've just seen a black-winged lovebird." The Kudu gave an affectionate snort.

"We have a rich variety of birds here, that's for sure," he told Bella. "And I think you'll find that most of the animals of the forests are delighted to see you."

Bella was happy to hear this but was anxious to be making headway with her journey.

"I need to get to Lake Tana as quickly as I can," she told the Kudu.

He sighed, gravely. "Between here and Lake Tana stand the Simian Mountains. So unless you can fly – which I don't advise under the circumstances – I'm afraid you have, at best, an arduous two-day trek ahead of you. A trek during which every wolf in the mountains will be out to rip you to shreds."

Bella felt her stomach lurch with fear. Even if the sky wasn't being patrolled by raptors, she wasn't at all confident about the idea of flying without her pendant. "I should never have left without the Quetzal," she scolded herself. "I'm too impulsive." Bella yearned to be home, to feel the warmth of her mum's smile and taste one of her delicious home-baked cakes.

The Kudu stopped to rest by a small rock pool in a

particularly dense part of the forest.

"You need refreshment," he told her, dropping to his knees to allow Bella to dismount.

The Kudu's over-heated body emanated clouds of steam. Bella was aware that she too was sweaty and in need of a serious wash. She drank avidly from the pool, scooping some of the water into her hands to wash her face and clean her wounds.

"I had a pendant," she told the Kudu, wincing at the painful sting in her arm as she wiped away the grime. "I could have used it to heal my wounds. Without it, I'm nothing more than an ordinary twelve-year-old girl."

Bella was shocked by the disappointment etched on the Kudu's face.

"Is that what you really think?" he retorted. "What about the way you fought those wild dogs as if your injuries were nothing more than a scratch from a thistle?"

"But that was my anger," Bella told him. "I can forget who I am and what I'm doing when I get cross."

"Forget who you are?" asked the Kudu, becoming riled. "Or at long last, remember?"

The Kudu's irritated remark was confusing to Bella.

"Your anger and your passion are your greatest weapons," the Kudu went on. "Anyone can see that." Then, after a moment's pause: "Perhaps they are also your biggest weaknesses?"

A mad flurry of activity in the undergrowth alerted Bella to the feast of berries and nuts at her feet as ants, termites, mice, moles, rabbits, raccoons, geckoes, chameleons – even the odd snake – hurried to deliver their gifts.

"Eat," said the Kudu. "It might be days before you get to

eat with your father."

Despite his concerns for Bella's well-being, Bella was touched by the Kudu's confidence in the journey ahead and she ate heartily. After her meal, the Kudu encouraged her to sleep.

"It's daylight out there now," he told her, lying down in the leaves alongside her. "Your journey through the mountain starts at dusk tonight."

Bella snuggled up inside Mahlet's sackcloth shawl and nestled herself up against the Kudu's warm, soft hide. She was too exhausted for even her worries to keep her from sleep now.

CHAPTER TWELVE

NIGHT BRIEFING

Bella felt something warm and bristly nuzzling her nose.

"It's dusk," the Kudu whispered.

She pulled herself up and rubbed her eyes. All around her, a thousand pairs of eyes stared at her with anticipation.

"So this is the girl," squawked a beautiful parrot with a dazzling yellow chest. For a second, Bella's heart jumped with joy, thinking he was the Quetzal. When she realized her mistake she felt sad.

"How's your arm?" asked a scruffy little mole rat. Bella examined her injured arm and found that it was wrapped in moist green leaves and bound with vines. Remarkably, she felt no pain at all from any of her injuries.

"It feels much better, thank you," she said, rotating her arm through a series of fencing warm-ups.

"We used oils and herbs from the forest," said the mole rat, clearly quite pleased with his work.

Peering up through the trees Bella saw the first shimmers of the Milky Way.

"Don't think about what you might or might not be able to do without the pendant," the Kudu began. Bella sensed by his stern expression that he was about to tell her something important. "Listen to your inner voices," he went on. "It's your instincts and your power that will determine the outcome of this battle – not those of a fancy trinket from the past." But Bella couldn't help it. She felt lost without the pendant.

"But why me?" Bella pleaded. A tiny white field mouse skittered through the undergrowth and clambered up onto Bella's trainer.

"It's because of everything you are," she squeaked.

"With the aspiration and powers of your parents, together with your own unique spirit, you can unite us all, humans and animals alike with one voice," said the Kudu. Bella found it hard uniting ten other girls in a football match, let alone all the humans and animals in the world.

"And how am I supposed to know about the aspiration and powers of my parents when I haven't even met them?" she demanded.

"You are the girl from the ancient prophesies," interjected a brown-skinned gecko sitting on a rock. "Call it animal instinct, but we all sense it. I'd run to your father's meeting myself if I thought my little legs could get me there on time." A number of other creatures muttered similar thoughts.

"Right," said the Kudu, trying to move things along. "I need to brief you about your journey." Bella looked up resignedly. "Go on," she said.

"The baboons will hound you," he began. "They're boisterous and irritating but will neither harm nor help you on your journey."

"We birds want to help you," chirped the lovebird, "but the raptors are killing anything that flies in the open."

"The owls will scrutinize your every move," the Kudu went on. "But they want no part in this war."

"Basically," said Bella rather abruptly, "what you're trying to tell me is that I'm on my own." The Kudu shook his head gravely.

"Not exactly," he whispered. Bella felt the hairs on the back of her neck prick up. "There's the Ky Kebero."

There were awkward shuffles amongst the animals.

"The Red Wolf?" Bella queried.

"The Ky Kebero may be rare, but they are killers," the Kudu hushed. "Karpov has done everything in his power to engage their absolute loyalty." Bella's head dropped to her chest.

"So I'll be pecked to death if I fly and mauled if I walk," she muttered. Even the crickets were still now.

"Something like that," said the Kudu quietly. "But you never know. Allegiances in this conflict are fragile. Nothing – and I mean nothing – is set in stone. The battle has begun. How it will turn out, no one can be certain."

Nothing the Kudu said brought any comfort to Bella. The forces out to get her were terrifying and yet here she was, setting out to walk right into the open with nothing but her wits and a few words of advice to guide her. The Kudu turned around and began to walk away. "Follow me quickly," he called. "Time isn't on our side."

As Bella sloped off after the Kudu she was followed by the sound of fluttering wings and a mad scramble through the undergrowth. She wondered how, without the power of the pendant, she stood any chance alone on the mountains at night. "Quetzal, I need you," she started to chant to herself. "I need you now!"

By the time they made it to the outskirts of the woods, the last rays of sunlight were dissolving into the night sky. Before her were the reddened, angular rocks of the Simian Mountains. Stretching out for miles, the jagged peaks and interlocking valleys looked so impenetrable by foot, they almost drained her will to go on.

"Keep the North Star behind you and you can't go far wrong," said the Kudu, making sure that Bella was still safely under cover. "The mountains are crossed by a network of tracks used by locals to pass between villages and herd livestock. Ignore the pathways and keep heading south. With luck, the raptors will think you're nothing more than a local girl journeying home from a neighbouring village."

"But look at me!" cried Bella, opening her shawl to reveal her shirt and jeans.

"Keep yourself covered," the Kudu huffed. "And stop being so negative. The town of Bahir Dar lies directly to the south. It's surrounded by mountains but the eastern side of town borders Lake Tana itself. From there, you will need to take charge of a boat, for your father hides away in one of the tiny villages surrounding the lake."

The thought of her father was a massive spur to Bella. Unfortunately, the feeling was short-lived. "I have one more thing to warn you about," the Kudu whispered, bending down to Bella's ear. "In these mountains, there patrols one wolf from the Ky Kebero breed who, above all others, stands out from his race. The other wolves call him Tila, 'The Shadow'. For years no one sees him, and then, as if from nowhere, he's back and killing anything that crosses his path." Bella gave the Kudu a helpless glare.

"I don't suppose there's any chance that Tila is away on one of his little trips, is there?"

"He's back." The Kudu mouthed the words so softly, Bella had to lip-read.

"How will I know it's him?" asked Bella, withering at the thought.

"He wears a black, spike-studded collar," said the Kudu.

"But that's what domesticated pets wear," replied Bella, wondering what kind of person would keep such a beast. And then, it occurred to her.

"Karpov," she gasped. The Kudu nodded forlornly.

For comfort, Bella closed her eyes and tried to imagine what her father might be doing. She saw him in her mind pacing nervously up and down a sandy beach. "He looks anxious," she thought. "And so alone." Bella wanted to be with him so much. To have him hold her in his arms and tell her how much he loved her. To tell her how wonderful her mother was. Everything! "Why is this so hard?" she thought. She was starting to feel angry now. There'd been an injustice in her life that had torn her away from her family, her culture – everything that mattered – and the weight of it was becoming too much to bear.

"Haven't you anything nice to say to me before I go?" she demanded. As her fury began to spiral out of control there was a small but tangible rumble in the earth that startled both of them.

"You have more influence over the elements than you might yet know," the Kudu observed. The sound of crashing rocks somewhere, way off in the distance, caused Bella's skin to erupt in goose bumps. She looked at the Kudu as he pulled himself up tall. "Goodbye, Bella," he said kindly.

Bella took a long last look at the mighty beast.

"Thank you," she told him. "You saved my life. I'm so sorry about Nyala."

The Kudu slowly turned and walked back into the woods leaving Bella to face her journey alone.

Well, perhaps not completely alone.

CHAPTER THIRTEEN

TRACKED

With a full moon almost directly above and the North Star shining brightly in the sky behind her, Bella began her trek into the long, dry grass that skirted the edge of the forest. The sweet smell of eucalyptus soon gave way to the comforting aroma of the coffee trees planted by a nearby community. It reminded her instantly of Lalibela and her friends, Yohanis and Mahlet.

"They must be having that meeting about the fair trade cooperative tonight," she thought, irritated that she hadn't had an opportunity to warn them about Mr Letellier's presence in the crater. "I hope Yohanis has the courage to speak out against the Corporation."

She thought too about General Karpov, considering not only his awesome physical presence and power but the fact that his own wolf might even now be tracking her down. "He knows I was at the crater," she thought. "And he'll feel exposed. I've seen his army and I know his intentions."

The thought of all the dangers that lay ahead was overwhelming. Still, Bella tried to keep a positive outlook.

"At least there are no raptors around," she thought, surprised that the sky was clear – at least for now. The chirps of crickets and the buzz of mosquitoes actually brought her comfort, while at her feet the scurry of mice and mole rats almost made her smile. Bella had always been happiest out in the open, surrounded by nature. The only difference now was that her relationship with nature wasn't quite as straightforward as it once had been.

"Clearly not everything in the natural world is on our side," she mused. She scoured the landscape for signs of wolves but there were none.

A fox by the edge of a field full of long, wavy tef stalks gave Bella a wry smile then darted for cover. A bushbuck, peeping up over a large flowering shrub gave her a non-committal snort, while a small herd of zebra grazing on the escarpment seemed completely ambivalent to her presence.

"I had no idea all these animals could be found in Ethiopia," Bella marvelled. "Usually, when Ethiopia is on television it's all about drought and famine." Bella had always wanted to go on an African safari and now here she was. She knew also that most Africans understood the word 'safari' to mean 'journey', and she had no doubt that she was on the journey of her life. Despite the rich diversity of animal life around her, very few seemed to be aware of her presence. "Most animals are too busy getting on with their lives to even notice you," the Kudu had told her. "It's just as well," thought Bella now. "Anonymity is my best defence on this journey."

Through beautiful alpine meadows lit by the full moon and glittering Milky Way, Bella journeyed on. Slowly, the lushness of the fields gave way to scrub land, where only the occasional anthill and acacia tree left any mark on the landscape. As she climbed higher, the muddy tracks turned to stony paths and gradients that continually felt more arduous and steep with every stride. Along a ridge half a mile to the east, a trail of twenty or so villagers, laden with sacks and bundles of wood, gave her a courteous wave. Bella wrapped Mahlet's shawl tightly around her body, thankful that they were too far away to speak.

Keeping the North Star behind her, Bella cut her own pathway through the mountains. While the route was direct, it was much harder to navigate the rocky terrain. Twice now, a swooping owl had made her jump and lose her footing.

"Mind where you're going," she'd screeched the last time this happened. As soon as she'd said it, she knew it was a mistake.

"You'd be advised to keep your big mouth shut," hooted the owl. "I can think of quite a few buzzards around here who'd happily give you away."

"Sorry," said Bella, wondering upon which issues the loyalties of buzzards hinged. "I must have more self control," she reminded herself. "I can't afford to be discovered here."

As the Kudu had predicted, Bella soon found herself being tracked by a large pack of gelada baboons. The long, heavy cape of their shaggy fur and grey manes were in sharp contrast to the bright pink skin of their necks.

"She's not from round here," she heard one of them yap. "And she doesn't look like a tourist."

Bella examined the deeply grooved lines on their dark brown faces and considered for a moment that baboons were perhaps far wiser than she had imagined. It wasn't a view she held on to for long. On a ridge higher up the mountain, two male baboons were engaged in a hair-raising chase. Running with their mouths wide open to display their long, fang-like teeth, the thud of their paws and their high, pant-like shrieks boomed out across the mountains.

"Show-offs," thought Bella, determined to keep her mouth shut for once.

The baboons hung around for a while, occasionally throwing stones at her and yelping for food, but they eventually lost interest and swerved away towards the last of the trees. The strange thing was, once they'd gone, Bella actually missed them. She looked back to the meadows, now some distance behind her, and realized that there were suddenly far fewer animals around her for company. What was more, the wind was really starting to pick up – a cold, spiteful wind that blasted into her face and made her eyes water. The rocks in her path were becoming increasingly more jagged and the cliffs ever more stark and barren. "This is classic raptor territory," she thought, peering up to see two black falcons huddled up in a crag, high in the cliff tops.

Bella was relieved to see that from a distance, animals clearly didn't recognize anything unusual about her. This was fortunate, because there were more and more buzzards appearing in the sky by the minute.

Even if Bella had felt the confidence to fly without the aid of the pendant, there was no way she could risk it now. But as if to mirror her darkening mood, the sky was filling up with an enormous, low-lying cloud. "At least the buzzards shouldn't be able to see me that easily," Bella consoled herself.

Perhaps it was the darkness and her fear of wolves, but Bella was getting jumpy. Several times, the howl of the wind appeared to merge with the wails of unseen predators.

"What was that?" Bella started as a break in the clouds briefly revealed the outline of a large canine beast standing on a ridge above her. The image disappeared quickly in a cloud of hot breath.

"Perhaps it was a coyote," thought Bella. She started to walk faster, even jogging whenever her footing allowed. Bella was sure something was following her. She kept glancing back over her shoulder, catching glimpses of a sleek, canine form.

"I am going to survive this," she told herself, feeling the animal within beginning to stir. "And I am going to meet my father."

It felt eerily supernatural, but as if to collude with Bella's verve, the wind that had been for so long lashing against her face was now directly behind her, ushering her along at an incredible pace. Not only was running becoming easier, but Bella's leaps over uneven terrain were ever more ambitious and sure. Despite this, there seemed to be nothing she could do to shake off her pursuer as the relentless rhythm of his paws tracked her stride for stride. "Perhaps he's waiting for me to fall," she pondered, tightening her fists. "He's toying with me, waiting until I'm totally exhausted before he strikes."

Bella had always been a fast runner, even without the pendant, but the kind of running she was doing now far outshone even her best form.

"The power of your will is a remarkable force," said a familiar voice inside her head. And so it felt. The beast was now following her so closely that Bella could smell the dankness of his sweaty fur.

Bella had just stumbled off the track onto rockier ground when suddenly it snuck around the outside and forced her back onto the track. She caught a fleeting glance at its reddish coat and wild, glowing eyes. "It's Tila," she shuddered at the sight of the wolf's spiky collar. A roll of thunder shook the mountains and the wolf picked up speed. "He's closing in for the kill," thought Bella in panic.

Before Bella knew it, the wolf was scampering right alongside her. With the sweat running into her eyes she almost didn't see the white mist rising out of the earth before her. "What is that?" she gasped. It was then that the beast pounced in front of her, forcing her to stop.

"Argh!" cried Bella, digging her feet into the ground. A huge cloud of dust flew into the air. As she skidded to a halt, Bella saw that the animal had landed a few metres away from a ridge. There was a momentary break in the clouds allowing bright beams of moonlight to illuminate the spectacular waterfall behind him. "I was running straight to my death." She just caught sight of the wolf's long black tail as he scampered away over the boulders.

"None of this makes any sense," she muttered as she walked warily up to the precipice and peered down at the enormous drop before her.

Bella now had the splendour of the full moon and Milky Way to illuminate her route and she chose a path that showed a steady descent away from the falls. Running now was much easier and it wasn't long before she could see the rooftops of a large, sprawling town tucked into the foothills.

"And that must be Lake Tana," she thought, at the sight of a vast expanse of shimmering water to the east.

Bella's heart was pounding as much from her joy as the immense exertion of her journey.

"I'm coming, Father!" she called into the wind.

Not even the mighty Kudu could have predicted Bella's speed at crossing the mountains.

"Perhaps the Kudu and the Quetzal are right and I don't need my pendant quite as much as I thought," she pondered, although she wasn't fully convinced.

From the northern slopes overlooking Bahir Dar, Bella explored the urban landscape. On the outskirts, the houses were wooden-framed and thatched, while those further into the centre were built of stone with sloping tin rooftops. Unlike Lalibela, which was lit almost exclusively by lanterns, Bahir Dar was speckled with electric lights. Bella's eyes were quickly drawn to the large enclave in the middle of town where powerful spotlights lit up five medieval castles surrounded by a high stone wall. The enclosure reminded Bella of the fortresses she'd seen in the tapestry inside the Church of Saint George, with the eight black-armoured knights and their freakish emblems.

There was a sudden howl from behind. Bella turned and for the first time saw Tila's complete outline as he leapt from the rocks above. She threw herself hard against the rocks and closed her eyes.

Bella thought it was all over, but at the sound of crunching stone she opened her eyes to see the wolf trotting off towards Bahir Dar. Her adrenaline rush drained instantly and she dropped to the ground.

"What is Karpov up to?" she gasped.

CHAPTER FOURTEEN

BAHIR DAR

Bella followed the wolf's trail through a field of tef grain to the outskirts of town. With still a full hour before sunrise, everywhere was quiet but for the bleat of goats and the calls of strutting cockerels.

"I wish my mum was here," she thought.

As Bella walked into Bahir Dar, she soon found it was much more developed than Lalibela. There were shops and electricity cables as well as buildings, some of which had signs written in English advertising rooms for rent. "There might even be some European or American travellers here," she thought. To add weight to this idea, Bella saw an internet café sign hanging up over a shop. "Great!" she thought excitedly. "A chance to find out more about Karpov and the Corporation."

Encouragingly, the lights inside the café were on. Bella ran over and to her delight saw that a young, white man in T-shirt, jeans and trainers was mopping the floor. She banged hard on the door.

"We're closed," he sneered, opening the door and giving Bella's dishevelled appearance a rude once-over.

"But I need to use the internet," she begged.

"Ten Burr," the man grunted, holding out his hand.

Bella guessed by his accent that he was British.

"But I haven't got any money," she told him.

"You cheeky little rat," scorned the man. "You come here at the crack of dawn and expect me to let you waltz on in and . . ."

"It's important!" Bella interrupted.

"Get lost!" shouted the man, slamming the door in Bella's face.

Bella banged her firsts furiously against the glass but the man simply pulled down the blinds and went back to work. It was then that she saw two young westerners with large rucksacks walking towards the café.

"Please," she asked, running up to greet them. "I need ten Burr to use the internet – it's an emergency!" The two men looked incredulous.

"I gave the boy up the road two Burr for cleaning my shoes," said the taller of the two. "I don't give money to beggars."

Bella had never felt so humiliated. She thought of her friend Randir. When she first met him he was begging on the streets of Delhi. "I didn't realize how awful he must have been made to feel," she thought as she slumped down on the kerb.

"You look exhausted," said a young African woman who emerged from the shadows behind her. Bella looked up to see that the woman was wearing a brown leather shawl and carrying a baby wrapped in goat's skin. "Come, my house is around the corner," she told Bella kindly.

Bella followed the woman back to a small stone house with a tin roof. Outside was a charcoal fire and several pots, while nestled into the coals was a black pot from which wafted the familiar smell of fresh coffee.

"You won't do very well begging for money in those," said the woman, gesturing to Bella's scuffed, yet clearly expensive trainers.

Almost everyone Bella had met so far wore either flip-flops or nothing at all on their feet.

"Come and have a wash and something to eat and drink," said the woman. Bella gratefully accepted a small bowl of water to wash her face and hands. "Who are you?" the woman asked, pouring Bella a coffee with one hand while rocking her baby gently over her shoulder. "You look quite unlike any girl I've ever seen."

Bella introduced herself, adding: "I've come to Bahir Dar to look for someone who might help me find my father."

"Is he a war veteran?" asked the woman. Bella looked puzzled. "Many such men come here after their time in battle," she explained. "And many wives and children come here with the hope of finding them too."

"I've been told my father is staying in a small village close to the banks of Lake Tana," said Bella as she sipped her coffee. Bella felt a little worried by the sad expression in the woman's eyes.

"Then you still have quite a search ahead of you," she told Bella. "There are nearly forty such villages surrounding this lake – some of them on remote islands. Without your own boat, you have little chance of visiting all of them in a whole month."

"Where can I find someone who might be able to help me?" Bella asked, refusing to feel defeated.

"Find your way to the Royal Enclosure," said the woman. "There you will find many of the locals who tout for work with the tourists. Someone there will be able to help you."

"Ameseginalehu," said Bella, getting up to leave.

"Minimaydel," said the woman graciously. "But please wait." She slipped her hand under her shawl for her purse and took out a worn, crunched-up note. "Take this," she said. "You'll need it." It was the first time Bella had seen the local currency.

"But you need it," protested Bella.

"No," said the woman firmly, pushing the money into Bella's hand. "You do. Go and find your father. Only don't expect too much."

Bella knew the woman was only being sympathetic, but her final remark was rather depressing.

"I am going to find him," she told herself, as she slipped the money into her pocket and made her final goodbyes.

Further into town, the neighbourhoods became more street-lined with stone buildings, some of them two or three stories high. Bella was enjoying a quavering, Arabian-like melody drifting out from a café window when it was suddenly drowned out by the driving beat of an old familiar pop song.

"Taxi?" hailed the driver of a bright yellow car as it sped by. The familiarity of the moment almost made Bella smile.

"Ethiopia isn't a bit like I thought it was going to be," she considered. Her expectation of sweltering, semi-arid plains had been swept away by images of incredible temples, luscious forests and beautiful fields within which a rich variety of animals lived. But there was more to the country than the stunning rural scenery. Here in Bahir Dar, Bella was experiencing a thriving, modern town. Another internet sign hanging above a café door spurred her on. She ran to the window.

"It's open," she cheered, seeing that three of the ten computers were already in use. This time the rate was five Burr for half an hour. Bella thrust her hand into her pocket and to her joy discovered that the kind woman had given her a five-Burr note. She ran in, paid the assistant and logged on. Typing

'Karpov' into the search engine, it didn't take long before a photo of Askar Karpov was beaming out at her from the monitor. A few minutes later and Bella realized the business interests of Karpov and the Corporation went far beyond coffee.

"He's into everything," she thought, finding links with all aspects of the food industry, car manufacture and new technologies, as well as a huge share of the oil and nuclear power market. "This guy's richer than anyone could imagine." Bella clicked from site to site, hunting for a reason that might link Karpov with events in Ethiopia and the wider aspects of his ambition.

"Five more minutes," called the assistant.

Bella connected to a news site posted only two days ago in New York. The page was taking a while to download and she'd almost lost her patience when the headline finally flashed up: Corporation to Lobby on Fair Trade and Global Warming. "That was on the news before I left London," thought Bella, recollecting how business leaders around the world were coming together to discuss the latest initiatives of world leaders in New York next week. "There's no way Karpov is going to be lobbying in favour of fair trade or global warming prevention," thought Bella. "He'll be doing everything he can to block them."

A photograph of a man referred to as 'American tycoon, Askar Karpov' surrounded by the eight most important politicians in the world emerged on Bella's screen.

"Why is this man in such a hurry to find me and my father?" she thought, pushing the keyboard away. "And just how powerful is he?"

Bella was about to find out.

CHAPTER FIFTEEN

BLADES AT DAWN

The medieval battlements of the Royal Enclosure loomed over Bahir Dar like a giant architectural impostor. As the first hints of sunrise touched the eastern sky, Bella turned onto the tarmac road that led to the main gates.

"Wow!" she exclaimed as the full extent of the enclosure's epic scale hit her. "Five castles!"

While small sections of the outer wall and some parts of the main structures were in semi-ruin, the general condition of the site was impressive. The mobile ticket office by the main gates was closed but despite the early hour, two teenage boys sat outside on wooden boxes chatting to a man on crutches leaning against the wall.

"Selam," said Bella as she approached.

The boys were dressed in the familiar blue and white of the national school uniform while the man wore a green army shirt. Luckily, the man didn't notice Bella's involuntary wince when she saw the bandaged stumps where his legs had once been.

"Selam," smiled the younger-looking boy getting up. "My name's Maaka and this here is my friend, Sabola. You're too early for the castle tour but I can clean your shoes if you like." He opened his box to reveal a range of polishes and brushes.

"My name's Bella," she told them, examining her scuffed trainers. "But I'm actually looking for someone who can help me find my father." Bella saw the man cringe as he turned away. "He looks so ashamed," she thought as she watched him swing his way up the street. "I didn't mean to appear rude." Then, to Maaka she said, "I need to find someone with a boat."

"Then I'm your man," said Sabola, jumping to his feet. "The owners usually ask for twenty American dollars a day and I charge a dollar to be your guide."

"But I haven't any money," Bella pleaded, "and I really need to find him quickly! I'm sure my father will pay you both as soon as we find him."

As Sabola pondered Bella's request, Bella thought she glimpsed a black and white monkey further up the road as it disappeared over a damaged section of the wall.

"Guereza?" she called, tentatively, breaking into a trot.

"Hey, come back," shouted the boy. "Maybe we can make a deal with the boat."

But Bella wasn't listening. She was already pulling back the metal fencing around the collapsed section of the outer wall and clambering her way into the enclosure.

Landing in the deep grass on the other side, Bella scoured the outer-courtyard for her friend.

"Guereza," she called. "It's me, Bella."

The morning dew seeped through Bella's trainers.

"Brrr," she shivered as she felt the dampness reach her toes. She looked around for signs of life but it was eerily still. "I have a bad feeling about this," she thought.

"Guereza, don't be scared," she half whispered, walking tentatively out into the open. Around her, the ruins of connecting passageways reminded Bella of the labyrinth of tunnels beneath the Temple of Tikal. She gazed in wonder at the wide, rocky moats surrounding the castle facades. Even empty of water as they were now, they presented quite an obstacle. "You wouldn't stand a chance," she thought, imagining the hell-raising fury that must have raged down from the towering battlements upon those below. The scene reminded Bella of that creepy tapestry she'd come across in the Church of Saint George in Lalibela. Then, as if slowly waking from a trance, she became aware of the sunken eyes peering out at her from various vantage points in the ruins.

"Raptors!" she realized with dread. She guessed there were around thirty vultures and at least double that number of eagles, hawks and falcons. "This feels like a trap," she thought as a growing sense of foreboding blacked out any thoughts of being reunited with the Guereza.

Suddenly there was an abrupt flurry of activity above. Bella looked up to see a raptor, so freakishly big it looked half-human, drop from a window ledge in one of the towers and clamp its talons around the battlement walls.

"They're like lawnmower blades," she trembled, imagining the ease with which its claws could rip through almost anything.

The muscular physique of its black, vulturine body, held in a posture of high command, gave it the appearance of a general in total control. As if all that wasn't daunting enough, it had a wingspan of at least eight metres as well as a long, scaly tail, which extended right down to a devilish spike.

"That's it!" thought Bella. "That's the creature I saw on the knights' shields – the ones in the Lalibela tapestry." She quickly scoured the ground for something she could use to defend herself with. "I need to get out of here, quick!" she thought, making her retreat. Then, with an almighty screech, the beast opened its wings and swooped down to the relic of a low-lying wall, not five metres from where Bella stood. Bella froze. "He wants to fight," she panicked. "And I've no way out."

"Can't you see?" squawked the beast, wrapping its sharp, black talons so tightly around the wall that the bricks exploded in a cloud of dust. Bella's heart was racing. "Are your instincts so primitive that you can't sense who I am?"

"What do you mean?" Bella stammered, sweat pouring down her face.

"Run!" screamed a voice inside Bella's head.

Raptors were flocking into the enclosure from every direction but still Bella didn't move.

"Who are you?" she shuddered as the light grey feathers around the beast's neck dissolved into a long wavy head of jet-black hair. Bella watched in disbelief as the creature's body turned into the black-plated armour of a medieval knight.

"You're so disappointing," snarled the knight. "When it comes to it, killing you won't be quite the challenge I was hoping for." Bella recognized the voice.

"Karpov?" she quivered. Her eyes shot to the knight's face, largely covered by his helmet.

Other than her father, Bella had never met anyone who could change their form in such a way. Not even Diva Devaki, the great Indian illusionist who had such control over her snakes, could turn herself into her cobra twin.

The knight bowed before her, then removed his helmet. As Bella's eyes locked into the glare of Karpov's dark, hungry eyes, she felt the pull of his negative energy, zapping her strength. She turned to run.

"Tila!" Again, Bella froze in her tracks. The Ky Kebero wolf was blocking her path, his jaws drooling with anticipation.

"No point in running now," Karpov warned. There was a loud clank at Bella's feet. She looked down. "Take it," Karpov beckoned. "My little spy tells me you've quite a flare for fencing in your after-school club." Bella stared at the mighty sword. "Prepare to fight," Karpov challenged, discarding his helmet and drawing his blade. Bella bent down and picked up the sword. Around the enclosure the raptors were squawking in frenzied delight.

"How do you know what I do after school?" Bella demanded, struggling to control the sword's immense weight. The first rays of morning sunshine struck Karpov's blade, almost blinding Bella with its brilliance as he raised it high into the air.

"You really have no idea what's going on, do you?" Karpov grinned.

Bella tore the vine-wrapped bandages from her arm. Then, leaning forward with her right foot to mirror Karpov's stance, she crossed his blade with her own. "Stay focused," she told herself as she held her position without a blink. These were the fragile seconds of calm Bella so enjoyed in her fencing matches at school when she would try and psyche-out her opponent before the fight had even begun – usually with great success. Not so this time. These blades were real. Karpov's height, weight and experience – not to mention his armour – set the balance of power so heavily in his corner, Bella's chances looked futile.

"All this for a father who betrayed you," Karpov sneered. Bella bit her tongue.

"I'm not going to be goaded that easily," she thought, flaring her nostrils in a familiar gesture of defiance.

Bella had seen hundreds of sword fights in swashbuckling films, where the first twenty moves were so incredibly fast they were almost impossible to follow. Nothing, however, could have prepared her for the ferocity of Karpov's opening onslaught. With a loud, bellowing cry, Karpov launched his front foot forward, striking at Bella's blade with such power it was all that she could do to hold her own as she made the first in a sequence of desperate parries. The deafening clank of swords and the screeches of blood-thirsty raptors reverberated around the courtyards and towers. Bella jumped up onto the remains of a wall in a move she thought might eke out a slight advantage, but Karpov was soon hacking at her ankles.

"I can't get a single strike in," Bella panicked, with no chance of making a riposte. "He's too strong." Every move Bella made was defensive, while Karpov's extended arm and swift strokes swished with such devastating force, each blow to her blade sent a painful judder up her arm.

"I can't hold him off much longer," Bella grunted as she jumped high into the air to avoid a vicious swipe at her knees.

"Scale the battlements!" ordered a voice inside her head.

With no time to think, Bella leapt clear over Karpov's head, landing several metres behind him. But Karpov was sharp, launching himself up and spinning through the air so fast that Bella lost sight of his sword right up to the moment he launched it at her chest.

"Urrgh!" she growled, contorting her body just enough to dodge the strike and dive away. Landing with a roll, Bella was quickly on her feet, her sword and posture ready for action.

Having overshot his last move, Karpov stopped to gather himself and rethink his strategy.

"Impressive," he muttered, turning slowly around. "And without her mother's precious little pendant too."

"He's trying to rile me," Bella told herself, the sweat dripping from her forehead and stinging her eyes.

"Then I guess you no longer need this," Karpov sneered, reaching under the armour around his neck. Bella had to squint, but there, hanging from Karpov's neck, was the pendant, ripped from her neck by the black-headed jackal.

Bella hated anyone even touching the pendant, let alone wearing it.

"Control your anger!" came the steady advice from Bella's inner voice. But it was too late. With her heart pounding with rage she lurched forward to rip it from Karpov's neck and fell right into his trap. Jumping easily to one side, the knight whacked Bella's back with the handle of his sword and sent her crashing to the ground.

"They're right about your volatile nature," he provoked her. "You're too fiery and undisciplined. Of no use to anyone – even your father."

Bella dragged herself up and raised her sword only to have Karpov swipe it away with one flamboyant strike. Acting on instinct alone, Bella ran towards the closest fortress.

"I can do this," she thought, thrusting herself up towards a first floor window ledge. But Bella had forgotten about the wolf.

"Ahhh!" she screamed as its jaws clamped around her ankle and yanked her down into the moat.

"Hey!" called a man, scrambling over the enclosure wall. "Keep away from the girl!"

As the wolf dragged Bella up the banks of the stony moat, Bella was aware of a man on crutches, swinging his way towards her at great speed.

"Attack!" Karpov roared.

Bella peered up in horror to see a blanket of raptors drop from the battlements.

"Ow!" she cried as the first raptor sunk its beak firmly into her arm. With the wolf still gripping her leg, Bella watched helplessly as Karpov charged towards her, his sword raised high above his head.

"Off!" roared the man on crutches, swiping his way through the flock of harrying birds.

With one last surge, Bella kicked the wolf away and yanked herself up. But Karpov's blade was already in motion, hurtling towards her head with deadly force.

CHAPTER SIXTEEN

THE SIGN OF THE CROSS

As Karpov's blade came down, Bella screwed her eyes shut.

"Stop! You need the girl alive!" squealed a frantic monkey. There were other voices too.

Bella opened her eyes just enough to see the Guereza smack into Karpov's head. The knight lost his balance and fell as Bella's head struck the ground.

Now, when Bella opened her eyes, she saw the anxious faces of Maaka, Sabola and the war veteran. She looked around for Karpov but he was gone.

"Guereza!"

The monkey was limping his way towards her.

"So that's what you were chasing," said Maaka. He bent down to stroke the Guereza's head. "You saved this girl's life," he told the monkey. "You're a hero."

Bella flinched at the sight of the lacerations on the Guereza's body. She was desperate to speak to him but was wary of exposing her powers.

"Are you alright?" she asked the veteran as he lowered himself beside her and discarded his crutches. Bella rubbed her hand over her head where she'd hit the ground. Luckily, she'd not hit rock but gravel, which had a little give.

"Was that really a knight?" asked Sabola, sceptically.

"More like a wizard," said Maaka emphatically. "Look!"

He pointed high into the morning sky to the great, black-winged creature soaring away towards the mountains. Bella watched Karpov's departure with a mixture of confusion and distrust.

"What happened to the wolf?" asked Sabola, giving the courtyards a quick sweep with his eyes.

"Don't worry about him" said the veteran, confidently. "He won't return now. Not with all of us here."

Bella wondered how she could have considered that the wolf was an ally. "And I'm supposed to be trusting my instincts," she reprimanded herself.

"We need to wash and bandage this girl's wounds," said the veteran urgently. "And then I think we need to take her to a doctor." The pain in Bella's ankle was excruciating.

"You're very kind," she grimaced, "but I'm desperate to find my father." She looked down to the steady stream of blood oozing through the bottom of her jeans where the wolf had bitten her. "If only I had the pendant," she thought. "I could have these wounds healed within minutes."

"But you must report this incident to the police," Maaka told her.

Bella stumbled for a reply. In ordinary circumstances she would have agreed but she was in too much of a hurry.

"Come," said the man. "Let's deal with all that later. Whoever that man was, he's gone and I don't think there's much anyone can do about that."

He ordered the children to carry Bella out of the enclosure and along to a standpipe up the street.

"Now, don't you go running off," said Maaka, picking the Guereza up and giving him a ride on his back. "I'm sure Bella wants to take good care of you after all that you did for her."

Outside the enclosure, the roads were busy and several street sellers had set up stalls by the main gates.

"That man looks Maasai," Bella observed, gesturing to a tall man in a red and purple tunic as he got off a mud-encrusted coach further up the road. The warrior was carrying a long spear and wearing an extravagant mane-like headdress. Bella wasn't yet familiar with all the traditional colours and garbs worn by the other tribal representatives in the multi-ethnic crowd, but it made for quite a striking parade.

"Over the last few days we've had visitors coming in from as far away as Australia and Papua New Guinea," Sabola told her. "Rumour has it, the tribes are coming together to form a council to speak up for their rights."

Bella was used to seeing people of different cultures, even walking down the street in London, but here there were tribesmen and women from almost every culture and country she could imagine.

While the man with the crutches gave Maaka and Sabola money to buy provisions, Bella turned to examine the Guereza's wounds.

"Are you alright?" she whispered, beckoning her friend to come and sit with her. "Did you get attacked by raptors back at the crater?"

"Something like that," the Guereza hushed, a little overawed by all the attention. "But don't worry, I'm alright." Bella wasn't convinced.

Once the boys had gone, the veteran removed Bella's shoes and socks. Bella glanced at the tears in her ankle, expecting them to be much worse than they were. She had picked up so many injuries over the last few days it was a miracle she hadn't ended up in hospital.

"Maybe I don't need the pendant half as much as I think," she considered.

"Your injuries aren't that bad," the veteran concurred. "With a little antiseptic and some fresh bandages they should clear up in no time."

It was then that Bella noticed something that made her jump. The Guereza must have spotted it too, for his eyes had visibly widened, as there, hanging from the man's neck by a thin leather strap, was a red cross, identical to the ones worn by their friends in Lalibela.

"What's your name?" asked Bella, unable to contain her excitement.

The man looked surprised by Bella's abruptness and for a moment Bella wasn't sure if he would answer.

"Tilahun Alemnew," he eventually replied with a nervous smile.

The Guereza let out an almighty screech and for a moment Bella was lost for words. "What should I do?" she thought, her mind racing to Mahlet and Yohanis. She was bursting to tell him everything but somehow sensed she needed to hold back.

"Your family must be very proud of you," she said, finally.

She scrutinized Mr Alemnew's face as he washed her ankle under the standpipe. He looked troubled.

"You said you were looking for your father," he replied. "Did he go missing after the war?"

"Yes," she said, after a few moments thought. "Only we don't know why because we're sure that he's still alive."

Mr Alemnew nodded pensively. "Perhaps he was so badly affected by what he experienced he couldn't even live with himself, let alone the people he loved."

Bella had to think quickly and draw upon senses she had no idea she possessed, even with her mother's mystical pendant.

"But I need him!" she retorted crossly, hoping to challenge his decision to stay away.

"But maybe he feels that he will be a burden," said Mr Alemnew shakily.

"Well I think that's spineless," said Bella. "There are people in my village intent on selling the coffee fields he planted to a big corporation. It's happening everywhere!" Bella sensed the Guereza was getting impatient because he kept fidgeting. "I mean, what can I do? I'm only a child," Bella concluded. Mr Alemnew looked miserable.

"But people will speak out," he insisted. "They have to!"

"You'd be surprised how many people keep their mouths shut for a free goat," she told him. "But I know that once my father gets to hear about what's happening, he'll help."

"Got them," panted Maaka upon his return, handing Mr Alemnew the antiseptic and bandages. Sabola arrived only moments later with some bananas.

"Let's eat and go," said the Guereza. "We haven't got time to hang around chatting." Bella looked down the street for any sign of the tribal people from the bus, but they were gone.

By the time her wounds were bandaged and they'd finished breakfast, the heat was blistering.

"Thank you for everything," Bella told Mr Alemnew and the boys, "but I need to be getting along."

"If you haven't got much money, the best way of exploring the lakeside villages is to take the Lake Tana Ferry," Mr Alemnew told her. "It leaves at ten-thirty today and goes to all the major ports." He put his hand in his pocket and gave Bella a ten-Burr note. "Here," he said. "Take this. If you were my daughter and you came looking for me, I'd be proud."

His words made Bella sad. "If only I could make my own father feel like that," she thought as she humbly accepted his gift.

The boys led Bella and the Guereza through the busy streets down to the port. The diverse mix of clapped-out vehicles and bicycles, interspersed with ox-pulled carts and livestock, reminded Bella of urban life in Guatemala and India. As she peered down the street, she caught sight of the Maasai warrior she'd seen earlier disappearing around a corner.

"Hey, wait," she shouted, running after him only to find that he'd vanished into the crowd. Just then, a large flock of geese swept eastwards across the sky – the first birds of any species other than raptors Bella had seen in the open for a long time. "Something about this place feels safer," she thought, sensing that despite Karpov's presence at the medieval enclosure, his army had yet to get a foothold in Bahir Dar.

Holding the Guereza tightly in her arms, Bella went to the ticket hut and paid a stern-looking man in a black suit everything she had. They then forged a path through the crowded market down to the ferry.

"How far is it to the first port?" Bella asked the official in the scruffy suit who checked her ticket.

"It's an hour to Zege," he replied. "We'll stop there for an hour before moving on to Gurer."

"Come on," the Guereza yapped. "Let's get to the first village and start asking around. The sooner we find your father, the better."

Bella found the Guereza's company a tremendous spur.

Boarding the ferry was slow going as most passengers were

laden down with supplies. Bella and the Guereza made their way to the front of the upper deck and looked out upon the vast expanse of shimmering water before them.

"It's so massive it could almost be an ocean," thought Bella, suddenly overwhelmed. Dotted on the horizon she could see the tiny outline of remote islands.

"What if this ferry isn't stopping at my father's village?" she burst out. "I was supposed to be arriving by air with the Quetzal. He would have taken me straight to him."

"We'll find him," the Guereza reassured her. "We have to. And don't forget, your father has his own spies and allies too. He may well find you." Bella gave her friend a big hug.

"You're great," she told him. "I don't know what I would do without you."

Bella's affectionate embrace embarrassed the monkey who gently pushed her away.

"You and your father must have so much to talk about," he conjectured cautiously. "I mean, about all the secrets of your celebrated past. They say that between you, you have more power than anyone on the planet. To think what General Karpov would do to get his hands on such knowledge . . ."

Bella wanted to know all about these things too, but more pressing on her mind at this moment were the distrustful looks they were getting from fellow passengers.

"We shouldn't talk so much," she yapped quietly to her friend. "We're drawing too much attention to ourselves. Karpov's spies could be anywhere – even here." The thought made Bella uneasy.

They watched a cormorant dive into the lake and resurface with a terrified fish flapping in its beak. Bella caught the look of triumph in the cormorant's eyes and turned quickly away. "Poor fish," she thought.

Bella understood more than most how precariously the balance of nature hung. "One second you're hunting; the next, you're the hunted," she pondered. "Nature can be so beautiful and yet utterly brutal."

At last, there was a loud blast from the ferry's horn and a clank of metal chains against the deck.

"Am I really in control of my destiny?" wondered Bella as the ferry jerked away. "Or am I simply at Karpov's mercy, waiting for him to decide when to come in for the kill?"

CHAPTER SEVENTEEN

EASTWARD

If it hadn't been for the breeze, the heat on the upper deck would have been unbearable.

"I swear it gets hotter every year," Bella heard a young woman say. "If we don't get some rain soon our tef crop will be ruined."

Bella inspected the sky.

"Where are all these birds going?" she wondered, observing a seemingly endless trail of birds heading eastward towards the horizon. She had an overwhelming impulse to transform herself into her animal twin and fly right after them.

"What are you doing?" asked the Guereza, as Bella climbed up on the rails at the helm of the boat and opened her arms. Usually, all Bella had to do was wear the pendant and imagine she was a quetzal and it happened.

"Get down!" called the ferry official who'd checked her ticket.

Maybe it was the intense heat or the fatigue of her journey, but when Bella tried to take off, nothing happened.

"I do need that pendant," she thought, scrambling down to a chorus of grumbles from fellow passengers. "Why else would my mother have given it to me?"

"It's your instincts and your power that will determine the outcome of this battle," the mighty Kudu had told her. "Not those of a fancy trinket from the past."

But if that were true, it was impossible for Bella to comprehend how her powers could compete against those of Askar Karpov. The beast he had been able to transform himself into was so well armed and skilled it was difficult to imagine anything standing in its way. "And yet he backed off and let me live," Bella considered. "Why?"

As the strengthening breeze wafted Bella's hair around her face, she looked to the distant southern plains. At first, it was difficult to make out what was going on.

"The whole landscape seems to be moving," said Bella. The Guereza turned to look.

"What's happening?" he asked nervously. "I can't see that far."

Bella peered closer. To her surprise, her view was magnified even without the power of the pendant. What she saw was stunning.

"It's a herd," she gasped. "Thousands and thousands of animals all heading east."

What was so shocking was the assortment of animals within the herd: giraffes, elephants, wildebeests all walking side by side with zebras, lions, antelopes and leopards – and they were just the creatures large enough for Bella to identify at such a distance.

"Look!" screamed the Guereza, pointing to the choppy waters beyond the ferry's wake.

Bella turned to see several small clusters of silvery-tipped splashes flanking the boat.

"Schools of fish!" she thought. "Every living thing for miles is heading eastward." And then it occurred to her: "My dream!"

On the night last summer when Bella's father had come to

reclaim his pendant, Bella had dreamt she saw such a herd, migrating towards a rising sun on a distant horizon. But that wasn't all. Mixed in amongst all the animals, she'd seen humans – thousands of them, many dressed in the simple attire of farmers, shepherds and cattle herders. She remembered in her dream that she'd recognized the purple and red tunics of the Maasai, the short stature of the Pygmies as well as Mayan and Aboriginal men and women – in fact, almost every indigenous race imaginable! Now, as Bella scoured the view before her, she started to make out the bob of small reed boats heading eastwards over the lake. In one, she saw the Maasai man she'd seen earlier in Bahir Dar; and in another was a woman dressed in the colourful patterns of her own K'iche' tribe from Guatemala.

"I know where my father is!" she cried. But the ferry was already turning southwards towards the island of Zege.

"We've got to get off this boat, quickly," said Bella. "We need to head east."

Even before the ferry had fully docked at Zege, Bella was jumping over the barrier onto the jetty. She dashed past the bewildered stallholders waiting to trade with the ferry's passengers and down through the dense thicket to get to the beach. There, she found a dozen moored boats, similar to those she'd seen sailing on the lake.

"Don't tell me we're going to steal one of these boats," the Guereza pleaded, throwing up his arms in disbelief.

Bella had taken a pound from her mum's purse to buy sweets when she was seven. She got into so much trouble she'd never stolen anything ever again.

"I'll bring it back," Bella snapped guiltily, untying the rope of the first boat she could find with a sail and paddles on board. "But this is an emergency!" She pushed the boat out and climbed in. The breeze was rapidly gaining strength and the boat soon started to drift. "Are you coming or what?" she yelled to the monkey as she began to paddle away. The Guereza didn't move. "Well?" Bella repeated.

"I can't swim," he mumbled.

Up on the deck of the ferry, some of the passengers and crew were watching.

"Thief!" shouted one of the officials leaning over the railings. Bella saw that a number of people on shore were rapidly making their way down to the beach. Still, she jumped out and waded back to the shore.

"Don't worry," she told the Guereza. "I won't let any harm come to you."

"Promise?" he asked meekly.

"I promise," said Bella, lifting him up and wading quickly back. By the time Bella and the Guereza were safely inside the boat the first of the angry locals were arriving on the beach.

"Please tell me you've done this before," said the Guereza timidly as Bella unfurled the flapping sail.

"Never," said Bella. "But how hard can it be?"

Against a volley of angry pleas from men charging through the water towards them, Bella somehow managed to harness the sail and open it to the now blustery wind. Controlling it, however, was quite a challenge.

"Aieee!" shrieked the Guereza as he was flung across the boat, grabbing onto the side just in time. Twice within the first minute, the boat almost keeled over against the force of the wind.

"I haven't come this far to give up now," thought Bella determinedly, pulling the sail tight.

Then, as if the sails and the wind had come to an understanding of their own, the boat miraculously sped away, leaving the gathering crowd on the beach at Zege staggered at the gall of such a young girl.

"Isn't this great!" Bella cheered as they crashed through the waves. They were both soaked.

"I'm going to be sick," the Guereza retched, sticking his head over the side.

Thousands of fish cut a pathway through the waters, while in the sky an assorted flock of birds sheltered them from the blistering sun.

"I knew it!" clapped Bella euphorically. "There isn't one world for humans and another one for animals. We're all part of the same world. If we work together, there is nothing we can't achieve."

The Guereza turned to face Bella. He looked so sick and scared Bella's heart went out to him.

"Don't worry, my friend," she called. "We'll soon be back on dry land."

Eventually the wind quelled, guiding the boat into natural currents and an island beach, half a mile from the mainland shore. Bella watched the fish and the birds continue east towards the horizon.

"Hi, Bella," chirped a familiar-looking babbler, pulling up to pass on his regards. The bird looked tiny compared to every other species of bird Bella could see in the sky.

"I know you," said Bella with joy. It was the bird's spotty chest and rusty-coloured throat that helped Bella make the connection. "You were the bird who came to my hotel in Delhi last summer, carrying a message from the Quetzal."

"We're all here," twittered the babbler, hovering above Bella's head. "The Indian contingent is one of the strongest I've seen: kites, sparrows, lapwings, you name them – even that Great Indian Hornbill who nearly blasted you out of the sky is here." The peals of the Hornbill's maniacal laughter as he waved down brought an instant smile to Bella's face. The feeling of animals and people coming together for a common cause was very uplifting.

"None of these animals would be here if it weren't for you," chirped the babbler. "Now hurry along, I hear your father's waiting for you."

Bella jumped out of the boat as soon as she saw pebbles beneath the lapping waves. Picking the Guereza up in her arms, she splashed her way to the beach.

"I'm going to meet my father," said Bella happily, laying the monkey down. She ran up the beach and started to follow a path through the thicket into the forest. "Come on," she chivvied, looking back for her friend. But the monkey was in no state to hurry anywhere.

"Go on," he called feebly, as he flopped onto the sand. "I'll find you later."

Bella was too excited to argue. She ran up the beach and into the forest, pursued by an ever-growing trail of woodland creatures.

"Hurry up," squeaked a field mouse scurrying around her feet. "Your father's half out of his wits with worry."

Bella burst into a clearing scattered with mud huts and instantly she froze. Villagers everywhere were staring at her.

For a moment, Bella's heart was in her mouth. Then, with a simple nod of his head, an old fisherman tending to his nets gestured to a small hut at the back of the compound.

"My father's house," she whispered to herself.

Bella started to walk towards it but suddenly she was full of doubt. "What if he's disappointed?" she thought as she tried in vain to run her fingers through her wet, matted hair. Her legs were beginning to feel weak. "He's your father," hushed a warm maternal voice inside her head. "He loves you." She was almost at the door, when she heard a familiar voice that made her heart explode with joy.

". . . and that's why you should never trust human girls to do anything you tell them," it announced decisively.

"Quetzal!" she shouted, barging through the door. The Quetzal was so startled he fell off his perch.

"Ow!" he shrieked, as he hit the floor.

"I told you she'd come," said the spider on the roof.

"Quetzal, I'm so happy to see you," said Bella joyfully. But the Quetzal wasn't feeling quite so euphoric.

"Well stone the crows!" he squawked. "If it's not the world's most unreliable, ungrateful, unimaginably irritating girl ever sent to . . ."

"Here, let me help you," Bella interrupted, helping the bird up and brushing down his feathers. Clearly flustered by his fall, the Quetzal fell silent for a moment, just long enough for Bella to take in her dimly-lit surroundings. Apart from a bed and chair, there was little else other than a mat and a small charcoal fire.

"My friends' house in Lalibela is a bit like this," she told the Quetzal.

"Lalibela?" queried the Quetzal crossly. "How on earth did you end up there?"

Bella launched into her story but the Quetzal was too angry to listen.

"And look at the state of you!" he bellowed in disgust.

The dust on Bella's jeans and T-shirt had turned to mud and her trainers were so soaked and scuffed they looked ready to fall apart. "Why did you rush off like that?" the Quetzal went on, his momentum building by the second. "I said, 'Whatever you do – don't leave without me'. Are you deaf?" He was screeching so loudly now, Bella had to put her fingers in her ears until he finally stopped ranting.

"You never explain things properly," Bella retaliated. "You go on about meetings and dark forces and needing to be swift – then you say, 'I'll be back in a couple of days'. This is my father we're talking about." The Quetzal hopped across the floor and kicked a pot, he was so livid.

"It's always about you, isn't it?" he complained, jumping up and down. "What about everyone else, getting things organized so that you can step into the limelight and get all the glory."

The Quetzal's words made Bella think. Yet again, she was reminded that something tumultuous was expected of her. Something she felt sure she could never deliver.

"I heard that story again," said Bella shakily. "The one you told me about the human girl with exceptional powers." Bella was trying to remember the exact wording. "The girl was supposed to lead everyone in a battle," she went on, "the outcome of which would become destiny itself and the start of all mythologies to come." The Quetzal, too, looked uneasy.

"Who else told you this story?" he asked, calming down.

"Lots of animals including the monkey who helped me escape from Askar Karpov," said Bella. The Quetzal's fiery emotions seemed to drain instantly.

"You've met Karpov?" he spluttered.

"Met him?" said Bella. "He nearly chopped my head off!" The Quetzal slumped to the floor.

"You really need to talk to your father," he told her.

"Yes, I think you do," said the tall, Guatemalan man standing in the doorway.

CHAPTER EIGHTEEN

FACE TO FACE

Bella knew in an instant that the man with the long, dark hair standing in the doorway was her long-lost father. Suddenly, in contrast to every dream and preconception of how this moment would be, Bella was paralyzed by an incoherent jumble of thoughts and emotions. "I look so scruffy." "He's so handsome." "Why do you keep leaving me?" "I hate you." "I love you." Bursting with a thousand questions, she wanted to run into his arms and hug him with all her might but all she could do was gawp like a star-struck schoolgirl.

"Bella . . ." choked her father. "I feared you were . . ." He stopped and pulled himself up. "Quetzal," he chirped, clearing his throat and directing his eyes at the bird. "There are reports of large numbers of delegates turning away from the Gongora peninsula based on nothing more than idle gossip. Spread the word that the girl has arrived."

Bella heard something scampering over the roof. She thought immediately of the Guereza but was too lost in the moment to call out. The Quetzal wiped his eyes and ruffled his feathers.

"They won't be going home now," he cheered, looking chuffed. "This is the news we've been waiting for." Again Bella felt nervous that so much seemed to be pinned on her arrival. "And to think I made all this happen," he sighed, before flapping up and away through the door. "I really am a most extraordinary bird."

Bella examined her father's face. It looked a little older and chubbier than the images she'd collected in her scrapbooks, but the shiny silver pendant around his neck was unmistakable. "He'll be devastated when he finds out I've lost mine," she thought, fidgeting nervously with her collar. She gazed into his warm dark eyes, which like her own were tear-filled and bursting with emotion.

"Do you like coffee?" he asked, sweeping back his long wavy hair and striding over to the fire. Bella smiled and nodded. She had always imagined her father tall, and observed how he had to stoop so as not to bang his head on the beams. She sat down on a small mat and waited for her father to join her with the coffee pot and cups.

"We sat here together in my dream a few days ago," she thought, stuck with a sense of déjà vu. The image had felt as real then as this moment. "Maybe the pendant gives me the power to transport myself in ways I haven't even begun to imagine."

While her father poured the coffee, Bella admired his colourful shirt, decorated in the traditional K'iche' patterns.

"I saw Guatemala drew with Brazil in their World Cup friendly match," said Bella, enjoying the ease with which the K'iche' language tripped off her tongue. "You substituted your centre-back for an extra striker with three minutes to go and squared the match." She found that saying something, anything, made her feel better.

"You like football then," beamed her father, sitting down cross-legged before her and handing her a coffee. Bella smiled and nodded.

"I play every day," she told him proudly.

The silence now was more comfortable.

"Tell me about school," said her father. Neither of them was quite ready to ask any of the really big questions.

Bella frowned. "I don't like it much," she said, taking a sip from her cup. "I always seem to be getting into trouble." Her father nodded sympathetically, then swigged back his coffee in one gulp. "I've got a really good friend, though," she told him, more enthusiastically. "She's called Charlie." She paused. "Only we've had a bit of a fallout over this boy . . ."

"You have a boyfriend already?" Her father looked startled.

"No," squirmed Bella. "But we had this . . ." She wasn't quite sure how to say it. ". . . misunderstanding." Her father reached for a large plate and began serving the injera and wat. "You see," Bella started, "if you start secondary school and you're not interested in boys, some people think you're weird." Bella could see that this comment made her father a little cross.

"You should never worry what other people think," he told her, laying the plate between them and handing her a bowl of water to wash her hands. "If you try and do what other people want, you end up losing any sense of who you really are." Bella started to eat. Normally she flew off the handle when anyone lectured her like this. Her father stopped for a moment and smiled. "Sorry, Bella. I'm being a bore," he told her.

"No you're not," said Bella quickly, thinking: "You're just being my dad."

"It's only that, if you know who you are and what you want, you will undoubtedly make mistakes, but at least you will learn to develop your instincts," her father went on. "As long as you can love, learn, forgive and move on, you will never go too far wrong." Her father's final phrase struck such a chord with Bella that she stopped eating.

"I've got this portrait of a beautiful Guatemalan woman in the attic at home," Bella told her father. "She says the same thing to me sometimes. I think it might be the voice of Itzamna, the Mayan goddess." Her father was hungrily eating his share of the food.

"It's a painting of your mother," he said, dipping more injera in the wat sauce. "I know, because I painted it." Bella's jaw dropped. Her father looked up quickly.

"Bella, I'm sorry," he said, realizing he needed to take a more sympathetic tact. "I've got so much I need to tell you I'm letting it all spill out. Let's eat up and then we'll go for a walk."

Bella tried to eat, but her mind was in chaos. She replayed the moment inside the Temple of Tikal last December when she'd raised her lamp up to the wall, brushed away thousands of years of dust and grime and discovered the faded image of the woman she had recognized from the portrait in the attic. "This is Itzamna in her female form," the Quetzal had told her. "You are her direct descendent." As if that hadn't been hard enough to absorb at the time, Bella was now trying to digest the fact that by direct implication, the woman in the portrait was both Itzamna and her birthmother.

They carried on eating, immersed in their own thoughts.

"So my mother's been with me all the time," thought Bella, recalling all the times the portrait had not only given her sharp rebukes, but calm, soothing advice. Despite this reassuring thought, it was all a bit too much family history for Bella to take in.

They finished eating and washed their hands.

"Let's go," said her father gently, helping Bella up and leading her to the door. Suddenly, as if coming out of a trance, Bella was aflood with all the things she had to warn her father about.

"There's a man called Askar Karpov," she blurted. "He's planning a . . ."

Her father raised a finger to Bella's lips. "Hush," he told her. "I know. I overheard a little of your conversation with the Quetzal. I want to take you to a place where we can talk."

They stepped out into the village to find it crowded with locals clearly keen to speak with her father.

"Please," her father begged crossly. "Give us a little privacy." He held his glare for a moment to show the full extent of his will and slowly the crowd began to disperse.

"You can tell she's his daughter," Bella heard one women mutter to another. "The hair, the eyes – everything. They're so alike." That comment made Bella feel good.

"She looks a little small and scraggy to be one of those heroine-types," Bella heard an old anteater snort as her father led her into the forest. "My guess is we're doomed. All of us." That remark didn't sit quite as well with her.

"People seem a bit wary of us," said Bella, glancing over her shoulder.

"You and I are outsiders here," her father replied solemnly. "We stick out. Sometimes people don't like that – wherever you are."

The crunch of dry leaves and twigs beneath Bella's trainers reminded her of being in Oxleas Woods. She looked into the upper canopies, where at home she might have expected to see a friendly sparrow or robin, and glimpsed what looked like a black and white monkey swinging through the trees.

"Guereza?" she called, hopefully. But then all was still.

Bella's senses were soon captivated by the smell of wild herbs and fruits. She imagined what a great playground the woods would make and wondered if she would have time to explore them with her father.

"Not far now," said her father, leading her up a hill upon which stood a small, round building with a thatched roof, far superior to the houses in the village. The building had a cone-shaped roof with a wooden cross on top. Sitting on the grass outside was a priest wearing a gold sparkly hat and a long white gown, beautifully embroidered with colourful stitching and symbols.

"She's arrived, I see," said the priest, putting down his leather-bound book. He spoke in the language Bella had first heard chanted by the priests of Lalibela.

"I'm going to show her around," her father told him. The priest nodded and returned to his book.

"Don't be long," he said curtly.

Looking over his shoulder as they passed, Bella admired the ornate and colourful calligraphy of the text. The language was like no other she'd ever seen and yet she knew she could read it if she had the chance.

"It's written in Amharic," said her father, as if reading her mind.

They took off their shoes and left them by the door. Her father, raising the flame of a paraffin lantern, pulled back a thick red curtain and gestured for Bella to step through.

"Women aren't usually allowed in here," he told her.

"Why not?" Bella demanded, instantly riled. Her father smiled.

"So fiery and passionate," he chuckled, with a glint in his eye. "Just like your mother."

His comment actually incensed Bella even more. "Why did you abandon us?" she thought angrily, the words on the tip of her tongue.

Once inside the church, Bella was as mesmerized as she had been inside the Church of Saint George in Lalibela. Here too, inside this modest little temple, miles from anywhere, the walls were adorned with striking tapestries and paintings. Her father led the way, holding up the lantern.

"They're so beautiful," Bella remarked as they walked around the outer-wall, admiring the artistry.

The sense of her father's tall, powerful aura, set alongside the flickering shadows inside the temple's cramped, gloomy interior, struck a chord with Bella.

"This is another place where we have been together in my imagination," she thought. "I wonder if he ever comes to visit me in the same way?"

Bella might have dwelt on these thoughts further had there not been the distraction of her new surroundings. There were many of the usual images she associated with churches: the angels and hallowed figures of saints and the Virgin Mary and so on, but at an image of hell, where a dark flock of evil-looking harpies preyed upon those within, Bella had to turn away.

"I've seen Karpov's nahual," Bella trembled. Her father reached for her hand. He looked anxious, knowing that there were many things he would rather keep from his daughter if he could.

"And what did you see?" he asked her.

"I saw a creature who was not of this world," Bella replied.

Her father was silent for a moment. Bella half-thought she heard the sound of padding paws outside.

"I want to help you understand what's happening," said her father, too preoccupied to notice. He paused and lowered his head, as if resigned to all that he would have to reveal. "There are recordings here of a dark, historic mysticism, that has nothing to do with the Church and its noble teachings," he began. He directed Bella to the centrepiece of the temple, a rectangular turret extending right up to the roof.

"I've seen one of these before," said Bella. "It's where they keep a replica of the Ark of the Covenant." Her father was clearly impressed.

"I see that you have some of the pieces to this fascinating puzzle already in hand," he smiled. "They call it a tabot." He opened the door and held up the lamp. Bella peered inside to see a large jagged stone tablet engraved with hand-chiselled text.

"Don't get distracted with thoughts about the Ark," her father told her. "It's the picture above that holds the key." He gave Bella the lamp and lifted her effortlessly onto his shoulders.

To Bella's surprise, her eyes fell upon the same image of the eight black-armoured knights she'd first seen in Lalibela, only here the picture was complete. The damaged tapestry in the Church of Saint George had only shown a bloody battle before an enclave of medieval fortresses, but here at the foot of the scene, Bella could clearly see a large, roughly carved slab, around which the artist had painted a halo-like glow.

"They're defending the Ark," said Bella. "But who are these knights?"

"They're called the Templar Knights," her father told her

as he lowered her to the ground. "The eight knights who stole the Ark of the Covenant from the Holy of Holy Mosque in Jerusalem where it had been kept safe for over a thousand years. They escaped through Egypt following the Nile until they found sanctuary here in this village."

"The Ark of the Covenant was actually here!" Bella exclaimed, totally stunned by the revelation. And then it hit her: "The Knights Templar was the band of knights Mickey was reading about in the school library." She'd read about the legend her father was referring to when she explored the book herself, but hadn't considered for a moment that it might actually be true.

"The Ark was hidden here in this tiny village for many years while the Knights finished building the Church of Saint George," her father told her. "Then they moved it to Lalibela and defended it there for hundreds of years."

"But didn't the people the Knights stole it from try and get it back?" asked Bella, hungry for more information.

"They did," her father went on. "But the Templar Knights were by then too rich and powerful to be so easily defeated, and besides – no one had any idea for sure where the Ark was."

"How did they get to be so powerful?" asked Bella, expecting more tales of piracy.

"Shrouded in the mythology of the Ark, the Templars set themselves up as bankers, took control of the rivers and ports and totally dominated international trade," said her father.

"My mum hates banks," said Bella. "They're always sending us letters for loans we don't want." Her father smiled, knowingly.

"Bella, I want you to listen carefully," he urged. "Even

though we're talking about events that happened hundreds of years ago, the legacy of the Templars goes on." Bella was engrossed.

"Do they still have the Ark?" she asked, thinking of the ornately garbed object that Karpov had been so close to revealing in the crater. "I thought it was held in a monastery in Axum surrounded by armed guards." Again Bella's father gave her a look of complete bafflement.

"You're picking things up so quickly," he smiled. Bella swelled with pride. "The truth is, no one really knows for certain where the real Ark is," her father went on. "Certainly Karpov and his followers like to give the impression that they have it because it makes them appear even more powerful than they are." He paused for a moment, gauging how best to proceed. "Who are the eight most powerful men in the world?" he asked his daughter, deciding to change his tack.

"That's easy," said Bella. "The leaders of the G8 countries. They're having a summit meeting in New York any day now to discuss global warming and fair trade." Bella thought that her father looked sad because she'd disappointed him in some way.

"I'm afraid not," he said wearily. He stood up and began to prowl around the temple, obviously riled by the information he was about to impart. "To survive and flourish, the Templars became a secret society and went into hiding."

Bella guessed at once that her father's story was about to take a sinister turn. "Nothing good ever comes of anything when people make secrets," she thought.

"The original Templars set up businesses that expanded to territories all over the world," her father went on.

"Shhh!" called the priest. He was standing in the doorway, bathed in such blinding sunshine both Bella and her father were forced to squint and turn away. "Keep your voices down." He let the material fall, returning them to the darkness. It took a few moments for the stars dancing in their eyes to fade. A little shocked by the priest's abruptness, they sat in silence while Bella examined the chinks in the outer wall and noted how modest this little temple was compared with the massive rock-hewn structures of Lalibela. As her father crouched before her, Bella realized how cold she felt.

"Have you noticed how faded and worn the material is, particularly around the emblems on the knight's shields?" he asked. "As if someone has tampered with the original?" Bella peered at the freakish creatures painted onto the knight's shields – the ones that Askar Karpov could transform himself into. "A magnified section taken from any one of these paintings would reveal that the original artwork showed the emblem of the real Templars," her father told her. "Someone has quite clearly gone to a great deal of trouble to erase it and replace it with their own.

"But who would do such a thing?" Bella asked.

"A band of people who wanted to rewrite history in a way that glorifies their own image and purpose," her father suggested, hoping to make things clearer. "As you know, people, cultures, even species change over time. Humans with nahuals aligned to the mystical dark-winged creature so often prevalent in old myths and legends became drawn to the Templars and their cause."

"It's like that at school," Bella interjected. "We all hang out with people who like the same things."

"And it was the same with the Templars," said her father, picking up his case. "In time, their greed began to poison their souls. Some of them became so disconnected from their own humanity that they broke away from the main group and started their own secret society."

"So there were two bands of knights," said Bella, checking that she understood clearly.

"There were for a while," replied her father, "but in the end one of them had to prevail."

"But why weren't they stopped?" Bella demanded.

"Because people don't always stand up and fight against things that they know are wrong," replied her father angrily. "Because we're human and we're lazy. Because as long as we're all right we don't really care what happens to anyone else."

"Well I don't think like that!" said Bella.

"And neither do I!" affirmed her father.

"But what happened to Karpov's nahual that it became so disfigured and unnatural?" Bella trembled, wrapping Mahlet's shawl tightly around her shoulders.

"You've struck right upon the heart of the matter," her father replied grimly. He stood up to stretch his legs and once again looked to the image of hell Bella had noticed earlier. "It happened over a long period of time," he explained. "Many would argue the Templars started out with noble intentions and that it was their quest for wealth and power that started the corruption within them. As for Karpov's nahual, it simply got contorted over time as it shadowed his crumbling humanity."

"Please tell me there aren't any more of these creatures," Bella pleaded.

Her father paused to draw breath. Bella examined his furrowed brow and the greying streaks in his hair. "He's worn out," she thought. "There's too much riding on his shoulders."

"I'm sorry," said her father as he sat down on the hard mud floor. "Is this all too much to take in?"

"No no," Bella beseeched. "Please, go on."

"I'm afraid to tell you, Bella, that there are indeed more of these creatures," he told her. "The first recorded sightings of them within the human world dates back to the seventeenth century – the exact date I can't remember, but there are drawings – possibly by someone within this breakaway band of knights itself, giving their beast-like form the name rakah."

Bella felt sick. "This is what becomes of secret societies," she thought. Her father continued.

"One thing we do know about the rakah is that they would only wear their black armour and practice the old rituals in secret meetings. As humans they went into business and settled in countries all over the world. For any of the rakah to be appearing now in their first medieval incarnations suggests that my strategy designed to force them out into the open is starting to work." Bella was impressed and reassured that her father's plans were having an impact.

"Is that why you've decided to hold the summit meeting here in Ethiopia?" she asked him. "Even though it's right at the centre of the rakah's homeland?" Her father gave her a smile.

"They've been hiding away for too long," he told her. "It's hard to fight an enemy you can't see. You need to provoke them out into the open. The fact that the rakah are now dabbling with the ancient mysticisms and rituals of their past and gearing up to fight in the open presents great danger, but at least we can see them."

"How do you know all this?" asked Bella frantically, feeling scared at the thought of such far-reaching corruption.

"Mostly through the stories I've heard amongst animals over the years and what I can make out from my own research," he explained, standing up again to wander around. "But it wasn't until I actually heard your account of Karpov's transformation in Bahir Dar that I could believe we were finally getting under their skin." Bella could tell that her father was itching to get moving. "What I'd love to get my hands on is the Meleya," he told her, the passion oozing from his voice. "It's an ancient manuscript in which many of the rakah's secret traditions and rituals were recorded. Any inside knowledge of how the rakah function could really help tilt the balance in our favour in the battles ahead."

"But all these things you're talking about are in the past, right?" Bella blurted, hoping this nightmare of a story would have an ending that might ease her mind. Her father stopped and looked down sadly into her eyes.

"The legacy of the breakaway knights today is a group of eight businessmen that are all linked to the conglomerate they call 'The Corporation'," he told her. "They support each other, executing an economic policy that's strategic, ruthless and so utterly relentless it eats up all the opposition. Today, the Corporation is so rich and powerful that they literally control the world."

Bella recalled the picture she'd seen on the internet in Bahir Dar, of Askar Karpov as he socialized with world leaders in New York a few days before the G8 summit.

"So all the Corporation cares about is making money," said Bella, "regardless of the consequences."

"For centuries now the indigenous cultures of the world, thousands of animal species and even the planet itself have been pushed into terminal crisis as the world's economies expand," her father told her. Bella could tell by the flaring of his nostrils that her father was getting angry. "That's why I've gathered all the people and animals who have a vested interest in preserving the natural balance in the world. Ethiopia might well be home to the rakah, but it's also the very epicentre of the ancient spiritual world. Why else would the Ark of the Covenant have consented to be held here for so long?" The idea that the Ark itself had a will of its own was too strange for Bella to contemplate.

"So what happened to the original Templars?" she asked, trying to pull everything together in her mind.

"They became fractured and disunited, leaving themselves vulnerable to reprisals," her father told her. "They had so many enemies who soon set upon them, their demise was inevitable. It wasn't long before the rakah had complete control, not only of their business interests, but of the types of humans and animals you saw up at the crater."

"But what can we do now?" cried Bella, feeling as helpless as ever when she thought about such things. "I've seen Karpov's nahual and the rakah have such a powerful army."

Her father stood tall and clenched his fists.

"We have our own army," he said decisively. "We can fight back."

CHAPTER NINETEEN

CALM BEFORE THE STORM

It hadn't been the conversation Bella had expected, wanted, or needed – but at least it had happened. As father and daughter sat huddled together in the dim sanctuary of the church, Bella told the story of her journey since leaving London. Her father listened intently, his face clearly showing how proud he was by his daughter's courage in the face of such overwhelming danger. He praised and reassured her, as every loving father should. He told her not to worry about Karpov and his army; that when the moment of their enemy's attack came, their instincts would tell them what to do. He reassured her of the forces their cause could summon – that in the end, the power of nature was greater than anything the Corporation could throw at them. He outlined the summit meeting he was planning early tomorrow morning on the eastern banks of the lake, where he expected every animal species and nationality of humankind to be represented.

But Bella couldn't take it all in. Her mind was drifting. "Why does life have to be so complicated?" she thought angrily. "Why can't my father live in a flat around the corner and look after me instead of taking on all these other responsibilities?" Bella was also resentful of her own perceived role as 'the girl' in the ancient prophesies. "I mean, what do they all think I'm going to do against Karpov's forces?"

As they walked back to the village, hand in hand, Bella realized that they hadn't discussed any personal issues.

"And what about the secrets of our mystical powers?" she thought. "How do we connect to them and how strong can they be?"

It wasn't only Bella who was frustrated by these omissions to their discussion. The forlorn monkey, limping his way back through the forest, simply had no idea how he was going to conjure up a report that would bring him anything but complete disdain.

To Bella's surprise, before entering the village clearing her father stopped and pulled her gently towards him. "This is it," thought Bella. She looked into her father's eyes, all ready to say "I love you too" when he said the words she longed to hear.

"Challenge your preconceptions," he told her. "The creature who looks most like your idea of an enemy may well turn out to be your staunchest ally." Bella was confused. "There's one more thing," he whispered into her ear. "Something I want you to hold on to above everything else."

"Here it comes," thought Bella. "He's going to say he loves . . ."

"Keep your friends and loved ones close to you at all times," he said, his voice quivering with emotion. "But keep your enemies even closer." He carried on walking, leaving Bella standing by the tree, completely deflated.

"Why did you abandon us?" she called after him. But he was already talking with one of the village elders.

Bella spent the rest of the afternoon looking for the Guereza but couldn't find him anywhere. She was angry and upset that her father could tell her so much and yet couldn't say the one thing she needed to hear. "I'm tired of being angry all the time," she thought. "I'm fed up with bullies, I'm fed up of boys who fancy themselves and I'm fed up with waiting for a father who's too busy and preoccupied to make time for me. I'm fed up!"

Back at the village, Bella sat beneath a tree some distance from the main fires. She watched the women preparing dinner but became distracted by a group of children playing a piggy-in-the-middle game with an old Coke bottle. About ten children were standing behind a circular line drawn with a stick in the ground, with one girl standing in the centre alongside a bottle and a small pile of sand. The children on the outside were armed with a ball made from scrunched up banana leaves and held together with tightly-bound vines. These children were trying to hit the girl below her knees before she could fill the bottle with sand. It was tough, because whenever the girl took her eye off the ball to fill the bottle, she was vulnerable to attack from those on the outside.

"I don't fancy her chances much," thought Bella, drawn to the game by the laughter of the players. But the girl in the middle was brilliant. It took the other children ages to get her out.

"Such great fun," Bella smiled. "You can't buy games like that." She gazed around the compound at all the activities going on. One of the older boys was climbing a tree, collecting ripe mangoes and throwing them down to his friend while three teenage girls were returning from the woods with sticks for the fires. There was an old woman milking a goat and many younger ones pounding coffee beans and spices inside large wooden pestles. Bella watched her father as he knelt before a hen and muttered some words before picking up the two eggs she had laid. "He was thanking her," thought Bella, feeling her passions beginning to stir. "We have so much to learn from these people about our interdependence with nature."

She thought too how a fair trade company would completely bypass the Corporation and hoped that Mahlet and Yohanis had managed to convince their coffee cooperative in Lalibela. "This battle can be won," she thought, getting excited. "My father's right. We have to fight back!" She jumped up and went to ask the children if she could join in their game.

That night, after the children had all helped with the washing up, it was still too hot to go inside. Many of the villagers were already dragging mats out into the open or making beds out of freshly fallen leaves. Bella watched her father as he pulled himself up into a tree to speak with the Quetzal. Feeling a little rejected, she found herself a comfortable place to rest where she could see them. Her father appeared worried by what the Quetzal was saying. After a while, the Quetzal flew down.

"I've seen your monkey," he chirped, curtly. "He was hiding in a tree talking with a condor half a mile west up the lake."

"Great," said Bella. "Did you tell him where I was?" The Quetzal looked dumbfounded.

"No I did not!" he scolded.

"Hey," hushed Bella's father from the tree, just loud enough for them to hear. "People are trying to sleep."

"What the blazes was he doing talking with a condor, that's what I want to know?" the Quetzal demanded. "The last thing we need is a traitor this close at hand."

The Quetzal often said things that riled Bella, but the assertion that the Guereza was a traitor was hurtful.

"Guereza is no traitor," Bella objected. "How dare you even suggest it."

"No?" queried the Quetzal. "Then what was he doing lurking around your father's house when you first arrived?" Bella half-remembered hearing something on the roof. "And why was he hanging around the church while you and your father were talking earlier, only to sneak off into the woods as soon as you stepped out?"

Bella was furious, but before she could really give the Quetzal a piece of her mind, her father sat down beside her.

"Shhh," he hushed. "We all need to get some rest."

"But father," Bella pleaded, "the Quetzal says . . ." Her father put a finger over Bella's lips.

"I know how you see things, Bella," he told her. "Your mother also believed in the innate goodness of animals and humans alike." Bella wasn't so sure she saw things this way at all.

"But you didn't agree with her, did you?" Bella challenged, feeling an overwhelming surge of support for her mother.

Her father faltered, clearly thrown by Bella's affront. He looked deeply into his daughter's eyes, sad that he'd never had the chance to talk of such things before.

"I wanted to, Bella," he answered at long last. "More than anything else in the world, I still do. But what happened to the Guereza when you were making your escape from the crater?" Bella cast her mind back. It had been a frenetic scene.

"I told you before. The poor thing fell," she told him. "The jackal was all over us."

"But you didn't see the little wretch again, until the moment you say that he saved you from Askar Karpov," the Quetzal pointed out.

"At least he was there to help me, which is more than I can say for you!" said Bella.

Bella's father reached out and clamped the Quetzal's beak closed with his right hand.

"Tell me again exactly what happened," her father urged. "Anything the Guereza may have said." Bella wasn't sure if the Quetzal was turning red with rage or because he needed to breathe. Still, it was a relief not to have to deal with his incessant badgering. She racked her brains to try and answer her father's question.

"He threw himself at Karpov's head," she told him, replaying the Guereza's heroic actions in her mind. "He cried, 'stop'," she told them. "'You need the girl alive'."

"Told you," gasped the Quetzal, the second Bella's father released his grip.

Everyone was still. The silence made Bella feel uneasy. "I suppose it was a strange thing to say," she thought. And then it hit her.

"Karpov kept me alive so I would lead him straight to you, didn't he?" she mumbled. No one spoke for a full minute.

In her mind, Bella replayed Karpov's speech at the crater. "I want to know everything that passes between them," he'd said. "There are secrets held by these two about the mystical powers of their ancient tribe that even we at the Corporation might have some use for."

"Karpov probably set the whole swordfight up so that the monkey would gain your complete confidence when he came to your rescue," said Bella's father, breaking the silence.

"Nice girl, your daughter," tutted the Quetzal, shaking his head. "Terrible judge of character."

"Off!" yelled her father, waving the Quetzal away. The woeful bird took to the sky. "This doesn't bode well," groaned the bird. Bella's father turned to face her.

"Luckily, nothing about our conversation in the church was of any use to Karpov's cause," he told her. "He's more interested in the secrets of our family and how we channel our powers."

What was meant to sound like solace to Bella actually made her feel quite cross. "I want to know, too!" she thought. "When are we going to get a chance to talk about these things?"

Bella tried to accept the overwhelming evidence against the monkey but she couldn't believe that he was truly evil.

"Father, I'm so sorry," Bella began. "You asked me to come and help and all I've done is make things worse." He put his hand on Bella's shoulder and looked into her eyes.

"You haven't made things worse," he told her kindly. "Perhaps if we'd talked about the things we should have, the Guereza might have had something worth telling his master. As it is, he knows only as much as I want him to."

Bella found her father's words reassuring.

"He's playing a strategic game," she reminded herself, "flushing Karpov out into the open where he can see him."

"But Karpov has so many weapons," said Bella. "His army will completely sabotage your summit." Her father looked up into the heavens and closed his eyes.

"He's praying," thought Bella, not knowing what to do or say next.

"Bella," whispered her father, opening his eyes. "Think of all the hurricanes, earthquakes and tsunamis you're always hearing about on the news: The power of nature is greater than anything humankind alone can create. And if it follows that humans and animals share the same world and lead parallel lives, we just need someone who can unite us in the same way that Karpov has done with his own army. If every individual we speak to tomorrow goes back home and has an impact for our cause – even in the tiniest of ways – the word will spread. If this happens in enough places, Karpov and the Corporation will ultimately fail."

Bella nodded – she knew her father was right. She was also sure that many of those gathered at the crater could be persuaded to join their cause if only they could be shown how destructive the rakah's greed had become.

"You are that girl, Bella," her father added. "The one from the ancient prophesy."

"But I'm twelve," Bella implored. "What can I do?"

Her father smiled. "Like I told you, Bella. We will both know what to do when the time comes. Just remember everything I've told you, and know this: I love you. I love you, no matter what happens."

His words drifted into Bella's ears and cut straight to her heart. She threw herself into his arms and hugged him tighter than she'd ever hugged anyone.

"I love you too, Father," she sobbed. She held him for a long time as the memory of his words replayed in her head, again and again. "'I love you. I love you, no matter what happens . . .'"

Eventually, her father gently lifted her arms away.

"We must eat and then get some sleep," he said softly. He paused thoughtfully. "Your mother taught me many things.

She would say, 'Everything that happens in all our yesterdays has its impact on today. But it's what we do with all our tomorrows that determines our destiny'."

Bella and her father shared a hastily eaten plate of injera and wat. Bella would have loved to talk for longer but frustratingly there were far too many demands on her father's time. Before she lay down for the night, she spent a long time exploring the stars and pondering her connection with world. Since finding the pendant, Bella's life had changed so much she sometimes felt disconnected from her adoptive mum and friends back home.

"One day I'm going to tell them about all of this," she thought. "It's not right to keep such things from the people you love."

While Bella's conversation with her father inevitably led her to think about her birthmother, she couldn't help but think of her dear mum, too.

"I love you, Mum," she whispered. "And I know you would want me to find out everything I could about my birthparents."

She listened to the gentle lapping of the waves in the distance and tried to imagine herself safely cocooned inside her mother's womb. "Did you ever feel like this, Mother?" she thought. "Was it lonely being you? Did you get angry about things? Did you ever feel frustrated because you wanted to change something that wasn't fair and didn't know how?" She also wondered exactly what her father expected of her and what she could really achieve without the power of the pendant. Then she thought about what both the Quetzal and the Kudu had told her about not needing it – that she alone held all the power. Feeling totally exhausted with all these thoughts bouncing around her head, it wasn't long before Bella fell fast asleep.

CHAPTER TWENTY

INVASION

Two hours before dawn, Bella was awoken with a sharp peck on the ear.

"Have a banana," the Quetzal squawked. Bella sat up quickly. "Tastiest banana I've had since leaving Guatemala," munched the Quetzal. "I highly recommend them."

"I highly recommend you back off!" snarled Bella, who was never at her best first thing in the morning – particularly after three hours of sleep on the rock-hard ground. "Where's my father?"

"He's down on the beach," chomped the Quetzal. "Waiting for you."

Their conversation was disturbing the sleep of those around them. Bella snatched the banana and staggered to her feet.

"Who else is coming?" she croaked, peeling back the skin.

"No one," replied the Quetzal, tossing his banana skin into the bushes. "Come on." He made ready to fly.

"Hold on," said Bella, eating hungrily. "I've lost the pendant. I'm not flying anywhere."

"Great start to the day this is," grumbled the Quetzal, starting to hop.

By the light of the stars, the Quetzal led Bella through the forest and down to the bushes at the head of the beach. There, they found her father clearing back the thicket to reveal a battered old speedboat resting on a rusty trailer.

"You'll have to help me push, Bella," said her father, tossing the last of the prickly branches away. "No one else will."

Further up the beach, a small crowd of villagers was following their departure.

"Why are they so suspicious of us?" asked Bella.

"Would you like it if thousands of people and animals from all over the world decided to have a huge meeting near your house?" replied her father, sympathetically.

Father and daughter pushed the boat out into the shallow waters.

"Get in and sit down," her father ordered as he yanked the engine lead. The surge of the motor was followed by the grind of rusty propellers as they stuttered into motion. Bella stepped carefully in, steadied herself and made her way up to the front.

"Aren't you coming?" she called to the Quetzal back on the beach.

"Boats are for wimps," replied the Quetzal snootily. "I'm flying."

"Hold on, Bella," called her father as the boat jerked away.

Bella almost fell off her seat. She clutched the bench so hard that her arms were rigid and the boat was soon blazing a trail through the choppy waters.

"We're heading for the Gongora peninsula," her father announced above the grind of the engine. "We should get there well before sunrise, akra arakiti."

Bella had heard the phrase 'akra arakiti' in the final cadence of an animal prayer inside the Temple of Tikal last year.

"Akra arakiti," she replied, acknowledging her father's prayer.

Around the boat a large school of freshwater fish cut a pathway through the choppy waters, while above them the long graceful wings of great white pelicans shielded them from preying eyes.

"You say this summit meeting is for all animals," Bella called to her father. "But what about the mammals that live in water and all the fish?"

"We've got pelican and stork messengers set to fly to all the oceans and major rivers of the world," called her father. "The Gongora peninsula is ideal, because the freshwater fish can gather by the shores and be instantly represented." A huge wave cracked against the boat, soaking them in cold, frothy water.

"Won't the big birds eat the fish?" Bella spluttered, picking up a small silvery fish and tossing it back into the lake.

"There's a twenty-four-hour truce," replied her father, brushing his long wet hair away from his eyes. "Even the crocodiles have agreed to it."

The morning sun exploded on the eastern horizon. Through squinting eyes, Bella peered up the coast to see a large rocky outcrop surrounded by a mass of figures, stretching out for as far as her eyes could see.

"Unbelievable!" she exclaimed.

Every square metre of land was covered, from the foot of the northern mountains right down to the south, and then eastwards as far as she could see.

"There must be a million species of animals alone," her father announced proudly. "And delegates representing every indigenous tribe and country in the world."

While Bella could see that many of the humans were in tribal costume, there were also large numbers of them wearing western clothes.

"Why isn't this event on the news all over the world?" she asked when she saw that some of the delegates on the beach were wearing T-shirts that bore the trademarks and slogans of various environmental groups.

Bella had a hundred questions she was bursting to ask but the huge roars of excitement from the expectant crowd made it impossible to be heard. As the speedboat carved into the sand, her father jumped into the shallow waters and whisked Bella out.

"They're waiting for you both up on the rock," called a young Aboriginal woman who stepped forward to greet them.

The buzz in the crowd reminded Bella of the excitement she felt at big football matches, only here everything was twenty times bigger. A thousand birds, desperate to manoeuvre into prime positions for the speeches, took to the sky while the waters were suddenly alive with flapping fish. Around her feet, Bella felt the scampering of tiny claws as freshwater crustaceans fought to get themselves to higher ground.

"Mind your feet," snapped a tiny crab, scuttling sideways over Bella's trainers. Bella tiptoed carefully through the sand.

"It's bad enough thinking I might have to make a speech," she thought, "let alone crush anyone who came to hear it."

A line of hefty bears and gorillas, chosen for their no-tolerance attitude towards well-wishers, held back the cheering crowd to let them through. With a guard of lions and other assorted big cats flanking their approach, Bella and her father began the steep climb onto the rock.

"Watch where I put my feet," called her father, looking down to check on Bella's progress. "A fall from here could be fatal." Bella was doing her best not to look down.

With a gentle butt from a grumpy old goat, Bella stumbled onto the rock after her father, provoking yet another tumultuous roar from the crowd. She searched the sky for the Quetzal, desperate for a friendly face, but couldn't see him anywhere.

With her elevated view on the northeastern banks of the lake, Bella saw that the crowd had been arranged in concentric bands. They were spread out from the rocky peninsula, right across the plains to the foot of the mountains in the north and east and down to the furthest southern plateaux. The big cats that had followed them onto the rock provided the first layer of defence, while around the foot of the rock a dense army of bears and gorillas stretched back several hundred metres. Beyond these there was a large band of tribal warriors, many of them armed with bows and arrows as well as spears. Some of these men and women had taken it upon themselves to bring through some of the smaller mammals from the zones beyond so that they could hold them up for a better view. After the smaller mammals standing behind the humans came the larger ones, methodically arranged according to their height, with the giraffes and elephants forming pretty much the outer circle while shorter ones got places closer to the front. To Bella's surprise, she noticed several wolves and hyenas scattered amongst the crowd, including one in the parade of large cats forming their immediate guard. She was about to speak out, when she saw the Quetzal fly over to a crow and welcome him into the circle of birds above. "Challenge your preconceptions," she reminded herself. "The creature who looks most like your idea of an enemy may well turn out to be your staunchest ally." Finally, Bella glanced back to see that the beach was now crowded with thousands of reptiles and crustaceans. "This is unbelievable," she gasped.

"Sit there where they can see you," her father told her, gesturing to a small boulder to his right. "When the moment comes, listen to your inner voice. Remember, it's your instincts and your power that will determine how things will turn out here today. Forget about the pendant."

"That pendant was from my mother," thought Bella angrily, watching her father take his own spectacular jaguar pendant and place it over his shirt for all to see. "At least with the pendant I would have something that showed everyone that I am a K'iche' Indian."

With long, purposeful strides, her father marched up to the very summit of the rock. In a powerful, theatrical gesture that commanded the attention of the entire crowd, he filled his lungs, opened his arms and roared:

"Ha – ra . . ." he was holding on to the 'ra' for so long Bella thought he was on the brink of passing out. Then, "Harak!"

It felt to Bella as if her father's roar must have been heard across the world it was so powerful, but then:

"Ha – ra . . ." echoed the crowd. "Harak!"

The sheer force of the reply shook the topsoil and sent stones skittering down rock.

"Ha – ra . . ." her father repeated, "Harak!" This time, he stamped his feet to emphasis each syllable. The crowd's response literally felt like an earthquake as a jagged fracture opened up in the rock beneath them.

Bella knew the word 'harak' from the tablet of stone she'd discovered at Tikal. It was part of an ancient mystical phrase so often used by her mother through the portrait in the attic to get her to calm down and think things through. "Harak, karadak, lopatos, almanos. Love, learn, forgive and move on." Bella's father was simply shouting, "Love!" The feeling induced by so many humans and animals chanting such a concept in unison was overwhelming.

"And so, the time has come," her father bellowed. "The day of which our ancestors foretold, when we must put away our differences and fight together in the most important battle the world has ever known." He waited while his words were passed on through the crowd by strategically placed messengers.

"But does the girl know what she has to do?" interrupted a warrior from the Kamba tribe, brandishing his spear. The warrior was buffeting his way forward through the dense assembly of bears and gorillas for a closer view. "And has she the power?" he asked. "I see she no longer wears her mother's pendant."

A murmur shot through the crowd. Bella watched the drooping of heads cascade through the gathering like a Mexican wave while her body tensed with anger. "How dare they talk about me as if I'm not here," she muttered. Bella felt the warrior was being disrespectful towards her father, too, by implying he had less authority simply because she'd lost her pendant.

"You all need to keep faith," her father lectured the crowd. "Only when the moment comes will we know."

Bella was feeling sick now with trepidation. "Another heckler in the crowd and things might start to take a turn for the worse," she thought.

"What news from the Americas?" enquired her father.

There was a scuffle in the crowd as a Native American warrior was swept along over the heads of the bears and gorillas to where Bella's father could haul him up onto the rock. The Native American's feathered headdress, like many of those worn by other tribal representatives, was spectacular, and his shield and spear left no one in any doubt that he would defend himself against anything that crossed his path.

"The news is bleak," announced the warrior soberly.

"Speak up!" squawked the Great Indian Hornbill, circling above the crowd. Bella gave the bird an edgy smile and a wave, then immediately felt stupid for doing so.

"Oil consumption and greenhouse emissions are at an all-time high," the warrior continued. "Our enemy's business interests and influence run deeper by the day. Asthma amongst school children in the cities runs at twenty percent and there has been a two-hundred-percent increase in genetically modified foods. Small farms and businesses are closing at an alarming rate as the Corporation swallows them up."

"Aye, it's the same in Europe," interrupted a Scotsman twenty rows back. Bella watched her father gesture to one of the gorillas to bring him forward. Within seconds the Scot was standing alongside her father.

"Wealth from the Corporation's oil business can be traced through nuclear energy companies, supermarkets, GM crop production, property development, fish and meat production – even football!" he reported to the crowd.

"And what news of our enemy's whereabouts?" her father asked, addressing the birds.

"The Corporation are thought to be establishing their new headquarters deep within Nemrud Mountain in Turkey," said one of the pelicans. "They've also bought land in the southeast of the country in a place called Kommagene – the land we know of as the Forgotten Kingdom." A gasp shot through the crowd.

"They desecrate the holy temples with oil refineries!" Bella heard one of the lions say to a leopard as delegates everywhere began to murmur.

Bella was quickly trying to assimilate all these new facts when the Quetzal landed with a thud on her shoulder.

"Look to the north," he urged. Bella's father, who was busy trying to reassert his presence on the crowd, gave the bird an irritated glare. Bella peered out onto the horizon where the blue sky was slowly being obscured by a gathering blanket of tiny black dots.

"Raptors!" she shouted. Her father broke from his speech and looked to the north in dismay.

"A bird of my size and plumage doesn't stand a chance," the Quetzal shuddered.

"Don't worry, Quetzal," said Bella. "Stay close. If things get hairy, I'll hide you under my shirt."

Word of the raptors' approach was sweeping through the crowd and the anxiety was clear to see.

"Why has no one taken heed of our warnings?" bleated an angry goat, through the hubbub. "They've been assembling in the mountains for weeks."

Bella looked to the north and east and recognized at once the relentless drive of wolves and jackals tearing down the mountains. She watched her father's body stiffen as her own started to shake.

"We must not panic," her father told his troops. "We are united. Turn and face the enemy." He called for the cheetahs to gather around him. "Send word to those that will be hit by the first wave of the assault that we will not desert them," he ordered, sending each of them away with a firm pat on their backs. Then, turning to the lions: "Lead the rest of the big cats out into the field of battle." Within seconds they were gone. Her father turned to the Native American and Scot and instructed, "Gather a dozen bears and gorillas around Bella and tell them never to leave her side. Then head for the battle front."

While Bella was roused by her father's commands to the ground troops, the battle in the sky was developing too fast for anyone to deal with.

"Helicopters in the west!" screeched a toucan, flying over the summit. "Eight of them."

The panic in the sky was deafening. They turned around and looked up. Over the lake, the whirling blades of approaching helicopters had caught so many birds off their guard that the sky was full of tumbling feathers and bodies.

"We've been set up!" screamed the Quetzal as he clawed his way up onto Bella's head.

Suddenly, from hidden burrows across the land, a thousand wild dogs charged into action. Bella was frozen with fear.

"Why doesn't the girl do something?" roared one of the gorillas, as the first wave of raptors began dropping their rocks.

"You leave her be," squawked the Quetzal. "She'll do her bit – we all will!" And with that, he flew off to join the fight.

"I've led them straight to you," Bella sobbed, running to her father's side. She looked up into his face and saw the desperation in his eyes.

"We were supposed to be flushing Karpov and the rakah out into the open," she thought in terror. "But we've walked straight into a fight we can't possibly win."

A dive-bombing falcon skimmed Bella's head and crashed to his death, while another plunged from the sky with an arrow through its twisted neck. Bella gave out a long, anguished cry.

In the bloody battle below, few creatures heard the distant roll of thunder that followed Bella's outburst.

Bella screwed her eyes tightly shut, her whole body shaking with rage. "The power of your will is a remarkable force," she chanted. "Control your anger and focus your powers." But time was running out. The helicopters had almost reached the peninsula.

"Black rain!" Bella heard the terror in the Hornbill's voice as the first droplets splattered against her arm.

"This isn't rain," she thought, wiping her finger through the black greasy splodges. "It's oil."

All around her, there was a pyrotechnic spectacle of exploding fireballs plummeting down from enemy helicopters onto the terrified creatures below. Within seconds, the dry dusty scrublands were erupting into sweeping fires, destined to burn and choke thousands of lives.

"Bella, we must get back to the boat," shouted her father as the first wave of Karpov's human soldiers began parachuting down. He pulled Bella's arm but she resisted with such force he was compelled to stop.

Bella didn't hear her father's continuing pleas to run. She was in a dark place now, alone with her inner voices, fighting to harness the powers she could feel rumbling deep within her. Suddenly, as if ignited by the realization of what she needed to do, she thundered up to the highest point on the summit.

"Bella!" her father bellowed, shocked that she'd so exposed herself to attack. He watched helplessly on as Bella crossed her arms tightly to her chest, raised up her head and slipped into a trance. He wanted to run to her, but he knew that this was the moment he and his compatriots had prayed for.

As Bella's head and upper body rocked from side to side, Bella had the strangest sense that she was rooted to the earth's core while massive bolts of energy shot up through her legs and networked to every particle of her body.

"Watch out!" called her father as one of the helicopters manoeuvred into position directly over her head.

Bella's eyes shot open. She glared with fiery indignation at the underbelly of the helicopter, armed to the hilt with rockets and guns.

"Show your face," she hollered. "I'm waiting." She would have sensed it was Karpov's helicopter, even if she hadn't already seen it at the crater.

The side door of the helicopter shot back and there he was – Askar Karpov – dressed in the black, medieval garb of his knight's clan.

"No!" yelled Bella's father, running towards his daughter as Karpov aimed a torch of burning oil at Bella's head. But Bella refused to jump out of the way, choosing instead to thrust out her fist in what looked like a suicidal gesture of defiance. To the astonishment of any creature able to witness it, a huge bolt of lightning ripped through the sky, fractionally missing the helicopter's tail. As the lighting exploded into the rock only metres away from her father's path, Bella suddenly awoke from her trance.

"Father!" she exclaimed, squinting and peering for his outline through the cloud of dust. Again, Karpov fired his weapon, sending out a jet of oil that instantly erupted into flames. Bella threw herself out of the way and rolled across the rocks just in time. The heat from the blast was so intense she had to bury her face into the grime.

"All this for a father who betrayed you," Karpov roared with laughter as he stared fiercely down from above. "And to think that your compatriots believed you could save them."

Karpov had tried to goad Bella before. This time, her anger was so intense she could feel her veins throbbing. Quickly jumping to her feet, she thrust out her fists in what she knew would be her final shot. As Karpov took aim on what looked like an unmissable target, another massive bolt of lightning tore through the sky. This time, it struck the helicopter's tail. A cheer went up amongst those defending the summit as creatures on all sides saw Karpov's helicopter spiralling out of control. Two screaming soldiers jumped from the hold in the moments before Karpov's helicopter exploded into the lake. But Bella's feeling of vitriolic joy was quickly quashed.

"Rakah!" screeched a passing stork, at the sight of the massive half-man–half-raptor beast emerging from the flames. Bella looked up with dread. She watched the Rakah garrotte the stork with a nonchalant flick of his tail then glare down upon the terrified figures below.

"Keep the storm coming," shouted Bella's father. "Let me take care of Karpov."

Bella was roused by her father's spirits.

"Come and get me," her father challenged, waving his hands into the air. The Rakah brandished his talons.

"But Father!" Bella pleaded.

"Just do as you're told for once," the Quetzal told her, swooping down from the battle.

"We'll help," called the Great Indian Hornbill.

Inspired by Bella's command of the storm, a hundred birds flocked to join the Hornbill-led blitz on the Rakah.

"So it's true," screeched a white pelican charging into battle. "The girl holds the power of nature in her hands." The flamingos and cormorants were right behind the pelican followed by an eager flock of sparrows and babblers.

With a thick blanket of dark rain clouds already blocking out the sun, Bella turned her attention back to the electrical storm. As she directed her anger at the enemy's aircraft, huge bolts of lightning ripped through the sky, sending two more helicopters crashing to their destruction. The strikes were devastating, not only to the raptors, but to the enemy's ground forces, many of whom were already turning back towards the mountains.

"Even the helicopters are backing off," observed the Quetzal as another streak of lightning was followed by thunder and pummelling rain.

But as the black smog from the bush fires below shielded the sight of retreating helicopters, what ought to have been a euphoric moment in the battle for Bella and the cause was turning into a nightmare beyond worldly comprehension.

"Oh no," thought Bella, peering through the smoke at seven more rakah, tearing without mercy into the terrified ranks below. Even the jackals and dogs were being swept aside, as if their loyalty meant nothing.

The rain was hammering into Bella's face. She raised her arm to shield her eyes and watched with horror as Karpov in his rakah form swept over the rock and made to bury his talons into her father's head.

"Watch out!" she cried in the millisecond before her father transformed himself into his jaguar nahual and pounced.

Bella was staggered by her father's ferocity and strength. Clenching the Rakah's neck tightly in his jaws, the Jaguar dragged him to the ground and began clawing at his face.

"Watch out for his tail," called Bella. But it was too late. With a swift lash, Karpov struck the back of her father's head. Bella winced as the Jaguar buckled. Karpov swiped with his talons, dragging them down the Jaguar's neck before thrusting him away with his feet.

"What are you doing?" bawled the Quetzal as Bella charged to her father's aid only to be knocked down by yet another rakah.

"Stay down," snarled the rakah, his feathers flattened by the storm.

Bella looked into the blackened sky where the seven rakah were still managing to hover despite Bella's torrential storm.

"They're waiting to see how this duel turns out," she thought, wiping the water from her eyes as yet another bolt of lightning tore through the sky. She picked herself up and was again kicked to the ground, this time by a rakah with blond hair and sparkling blue eyes. Even as she thrust out her hands to break her fall, Bella knew that something about his face was familiar.

"Fight as a mortal man," Karpov challenged her father.

Bella looked out from the summit. The battlefield below was a quagmire, but the conflict was definitely quelling as everyone turned their attention to the gladiatorial battle unfolding on the rock.

"Quetzal, where are you?" called Bella, searching the sky for her friend.

But there was no way the Quetzal could get to her, not with the rakah blocking interference from every angle. Bella turned back just in time to see Karpov transform himself back into the form of a medieval knight. Standing tall with his sword and shield raised, he made ready to execute the weakened Jaguar.

"Keep away from him," Bella warned, clenching her fists. She again tried to run to him but two rakah landed right in her path.

"Keep out of this," Karpov snarled. "This is between me and your father." The Jaguar whimpered. Bella could see that her father was losing blood fast.

"You're weakening your grip on the storm," warned a voice inside Bella's head. But all her attention now was on her father.

"Father, do something!" pleaded Bella. Then, to the wonder of everyone watching, the form of Eduardo Salvatore began to remerge from the panting outline of his jaguar twin.

"So you choose to die as a human," Karpov scorned, beginning his final advance.

Bella couldn't contain herself. She charged again with nothing but her bare hands to push past the rakah. But Bella wasn't the only one running to the Jaguar's aid.

"Stop!" shrieked a furry black and white creature, hobbling up over the rocks and onto the summit. Before Karpov had time to adjust, the creature launched himself up and dug his teeth into the knight's hand.

"Guereza!" called Bella, charging past the rakah as Karpov struggled to punch the monkey away. Bella was almost there when, to her utter frustration, she was again struck down into the mud by another rakah. She looked up to see Karpov clasp the bedraggled monkey with his left hand and drag him up the blade of his bloodstained sword.

"No!" she begged as the monkey flopped to the ground. She wanted to run to his aid but the rakah had every approach covered. Bella looked to her father. With the advantage forged by the monkey's heroics, he was now back in his human form and ready for one final attack. Before Karpov could regain his composure, Bella's father lurched for Karpov's sword.

"Ahhh!" shrieked Karpov as his sword slipped from his hand. "Someone grab the sword!" He looked up to the rakah.

Then, to everyone's surprise, one of the rakah swooped down and kicked it away.

"These creatures will kill even their own kind," Bella gasped in disbelief.

Karpov and her father were now wrestling over the rock.

"Mind the edge!" Bella shouted, realizing Karpov's tactics. "He's trying to force you off the rock!"

"You'll never make it on the other side," Karpov hissed at Bella's father. "Everyone will desert you, even your daughter."

Karpov's provocations struck Bella as strange.

"He's trying to distract you," she warned her father. "I would never desert you. I love you."

To everyone watching, Bella's words seemed to ignite her father's spirits. With both legs and arms he pushed Karpov so hard he cast him to within a few metres of the edge of the rock.

"Stop him!" Karpov ordered, looking up with bitterness to the rakah above. But it was too late. Bella's father pounced, and with one final surge pushed him right up to the precipice.

"Surrender and I'll let you live," he panted, his face flushed with the adrenaline of battle. Karpov, making one final attempt to kick her father's legs away, toppled backwards and fell headfirst off the summit to the rocks below.

The seven rakah were flocking around her father's head in a state of euphoria.

"Get away from him!" Bella demanded, desperate that after all her father's heroic efforts he was going to be mercilessly slaughtered. She looked to her father as he lay exhausted on the ground and was shocked to see how resigned he looked.

"They look more like a pack of adulating sycophants than killers," Bella heard one of the gorillas mutter.

"Run for it, Father," she called as the rakah moved in. She turned to the bears and gorillas lurking at a distance. "Someone help him!"

With no one around her offering any support, Bella again tried to run to her father's defence. But things were happening too fast. She was still several metres away when her father suddenly raised up his hands.

"What's he doing?" she wondered, realizing that he was looking her straight in the eye with such intensity his whole body was shaking.

"Harak, karadak, lopatos, almanos," he gabbled, as the seven rakah swarmed in. Bella's heart was bursting.

"Father!" she cried as she scrambled to reach him. But her father was already in the talons of the enemy and there was nothing anyone could do to save him.

CHAPTER TWENTY-ONE

AFTERMATH

Bella collapsed onto the rock.

"Father!" she croaked with exhaustion.

In the distance, the clearing sky revealed the menacing outline of the rakah flock heading back into the mountains. "So they've taken Karpov too," she thought as she looked blearily out at the two limp figures they carried. It was only when the image became so small it was indistinguishable from the line of the horizon, that Bella slowly became conscious of the weak, desperate gasps of a dying animal.

"Bella . . ." The voice was so quiet, the body so still, that everyone had thought the monkey was dead.

"Guereza?" called Bella, dragging herself up and staggering over. She knew at once by his drooping eyelids that he was close to death. "Guereza, how did you get here?" she whispered, knowing how terrified of water he was.

"On a log," he mumbled. "Paddled it all the way." Bella was staggered.

"You're so brave," she told him. "When you attacked Karpov it gave my father the chance he needed." With great effort, the monkey shook his head sadly.

"No, Bella," he wheezed. "I'm a coward. I betrayed you and everything I know to be true."

Bella didn't know what to say. When she'd first noticed the

lacerations on his body in Bahir Dar she'd attributed them to the attack of the raptors at the crater. Looking back now, Bella had no doubt what must have happened.

"He's been tortured," she thought. "Karpov must have got to him at the crater and forced him into some kind of a deal."

Knowing that every animal and human in the world had a twin with whom they shared an affinity, Bella had once looked into the eyes of Ted Briggs through the reflection of the Itzamna Emerald and seen a demented wolf. Now, as she looked deep into the Guereza's eyes and searched for his nahual, she saw to her surprise the outline of a young boy, standing alone in what looked like a school playground.

"He looks scared," thought Bella, who knew only too well how it felt to be an outsider sometimes. "Like he's the victim of bullying or something."

"Can you see him?" the Guereza whispered, a tear running down his withered face. Bella nodded, her eyes too filling with tears. "When I die, he's going to feel even more miserable than he does now, and he won't even know why." Bella knew that the animals were much more in touch with their nahuals than humans.

"He'll be okay," Bella hushed, shuddering to think of the tortures Karpov's raptors must have inflicted upon the poor monkey. "Somewhere, deep inside, your nahual will know that against all the odds, you managed to discover your inner strength and fight back. You're a hero, Guereza."

"Is that what I am?" asked the monkey, the corners of mouth trying to muster up a smile.

"You are to me," said Bella gently.

Bella waited until the image of the boy faded from the

Guereza's eyes before she closed his eyelids and laid him down to rest.

With tears running down her face, Bella whispered into the monkey's ear.

"Harak, karadak, lopatos, almanos," she sobbed.

She sat with the Guereza for quite some time before she turned her watery eyes out to the scorched bush land below where the last scourges of the battle were playing themselves out. Bella was in a state of shock and it took her a few moments to take everything in.

"So many dead," she stammered, as she peered through the thick clouds of smoke. The scale of the disaster was overwhelming. For miles and miles the landscape was littered with the bodies of animals and humans. Bella felt so drained of life and the will to go on, she wished she were dead. She curled herself up into a tight little ball.

"If this is war, I want no part in it," she sobbed. "There has to be a better way."

"Come on," squawked a flamingo, swooping over her head. "This is no time for self-pity. We need to help the wounded."

With a feeling of depression bearing heavily upon her, Bella dragged herself up and slowly made her way down from the rock.

"It's a massacre," snorted a limping warthog, giving Bella a disdainful glance the second her feet touched the ground. "We were like sitting ducks."

"Who was sitting?" quacked a disgruntled drake as he waddled by. "You might have been wallowing on your big hairy behind – we were fighting!"

When Bella realized that large numbers of animals and humans were dispersing at an alarming rate, her senses began to sharpen. She looked around for the Quetzal and found him sitting in a nearby tree attending to a distraught babbler.

"Where's everyone going?" she pleaded, turning her fiery eyes to every human and animal she could find. "We need to gather our forces and hunt down the rakah. They've got my father!"

"Shhh," urged the Quetzal, landing with a sharp snatch of his claws on Bella's shoulder. "They're scared. This isn't a good time to talk about a revenge attack. At least half of them think you and your father have betrayed them."

"Betrayed them!" cried Bella. "How?" The Quetzal beckoned forcefully for Bella to keep her voice down.

"Despite everything you were able to do," he told her, "the rakah and their supporters won this battle." Bella found this point hard to argue. "And more ominous than that," the Quetzal went on, "your father looked only too willing to go off with them." Bella was furious.

"They think my father has gone to join the enemy?" she spat in disgust. "He defeated Karpov – everyone saw that!"

"Are you two going to help or what?" roared one of the lions carrying the injured back to the beach. The lion's rebuke came as a welcome relief. Bella sprang into action, helping to drag one of the wounded gorillas down to the blood-stained waters where a team of animals and humans were busy cleaning injuries. With the gorilla placed carefully down in the queue, Bella and the Quetzal split up and returned to the battlefield. Bella helped a crab with a broken claw and a stork with a sprained wing. Then, to the surprise of a few creatures nearby, she rushed to the aid of a wolf with a deep cut in his belly after he was stabbed in the neck by a passing toucan.

"Get off him!" Bella ordered. The wolf was bleeding profusely from his wounds. "I need help here!" she yelled.

Bella didn't know on whose side the wolf had fought, but she didn't care. What she didn't want was mindless reprisals.

"Some of these wolves and raptors fought on our side," she shouted to those helping the wounded. "Pick on any of these injured animals now, even those of our enemy's ranks, and we are no better than they are!"

She considered how brave those birds, wolves and wild dogs that had fought with them really were. "It takes great courage to stand up for what's right when everyone else around you is pressuring you to do something else," she thought.

A leopard and cheetah came to help Bella carry the wolf down to the beach where the Quetzal rejoined her.

"So many dead," said Bella dejectedly. "A peaceful gathering swept away without mercy – and for what?"

"That's war," said the Quetzal, carefully picking out the stones embedded in the wolf's scars and spitting them out onto the sand. Bella bathed the wolf's wounds, too exhausted to talk.

"Bella," chirped the Quetzal tenderly after a while. "You may have lost this time, but you can still win the wider battle."

In almost a whole year of knowing the Quetzal, Bella couldn't once recall him calling her by her name, especially in such a gentle and calm way. "And what's more," the Quetzal continued, "you can do it on your own terms – without killing anyone – and in the process, fulfil the promise your ancestors made to the world."

"Do you think my father is still alive?" Bella asked nervously.

"What do your senses tell you?" asked the Quetzal.

Bella replayed the moment her father raised his hands for the rakah to grasp.

"He looked so sure of what was about to happen," said Bella, feeling rather confused. "Like he was still completely in control of his destiny." The Quetzal nodded thoughtfully, while Bella considered her father's departing words. "Harak, karadak, lopatos, almanos. Love, learn, forgive and move on." While it shamed her to admit it, Bella was aware of a bitter resentment towards her father, festering away deep within her.

"He deserted me and my mother," she thought. "And now he's gone and left me again!"

CHAPTER TWENTY-TWO

HOPE IN THE MOUNTAINS

It was late afternoon when Bella and the Quetzal watched the crocodiles sweeping mud into the mass graves. The steady dispersal of delegates had continued ever since Bella's father had been taken by the rakah. While few creatures confronted Bella to her face, she sensed their mood.

"And what happened to the girl?" she heard a snooty ostrich groan to a flamingo. "When it came to it, she was as good as useless."

The Quetzal had to keep careful counsel in Bella's ear to stop her from exploding into a rage.

"It's only going to make things worse," he'd say. "They're dumb – don't listen." But Bella did listen. She couldn't help it.

"I came on this trip to help my father," she complained, feeling depressed. "And I led the enemy right to us."

The Quetzal was having a hard time trying to make Bella see reason. "You think the enemy needed you to find this huge meeting?" he retorted sarcastically.

"People came because they knew I was coming," Bella reminded him.

"People came because they wanted to," said the Quetzal firmly. "Because they believed in your father's vision for the future."

"But they thought I could make a difference," Bella retorted.

"And when it came down to it, I could do nothing to save them or my father. Now everything's lost!" Explaining how she felt only made her feel worse.

"If you hadn't summoned up that storm, thousands more would have been killed," the Quetzal told her, aggravated by Bella's whining. "Now come on. We need to get going. You'll feel much better once you are home."

But even the thought of going home made Bella miserable. In a state of mindless irritation she picked up a pebble and threw it as far as she could out into the lake. It landed with a thud rather than the splash she'd been expecting.

"Hey!" snapped an angry crocodile, raising his head. "Whose side are you on?"

Bella threw up her hands in despair.

"Sorry," she called, then to the Quetzal, "I couldn't fly home now, even if I wanted to – not without the pendant."

"For goodness sake," cried the Quetzal. "Enough! Haven't you learnt anything?" Bella was used to the Quetzal being short with her, but even she was shocked by his stern rebuke. "You followed your instincts in the battle and look what amazing powers you summoned up," he lectured her. "The fact that you allowed your focus on the storm to wander when Karpov attacked your father was unforgivable, but hey – you're human." Provoking his human twin for his own ends came easily to the Quetzal.

"You're so pompous and self-righteous it makes me sick!" Bella shouted. The Quetzal couldn't help but smile to himself.

"She's so like me," he thought, as he flew up into a tree and gave her the most judgmental look he could muster.

"And what are you looking so happy about now?" asked

Bella crossly, flying up into the tree to give him the earful he so deserved. As she wrapped her claws around the branch, she could hardly believe what she'd done.

"Come on," squawked the Quetzal, soaring away from his young protégée. "You've been thinking about things far too much. Follow your instincts and know that it's the power in you and not . . ."

". . . in any fancy trinket from the past," Bella interrupted, irritated that she'd been so easily duped. "Why haven't I sussed this out before," she scolded herself, taking to the sky as easily as a duck to water. "I keep thinking things are out of my control and they're not."

"Shall we head back to London, then?" chirped the Quetzal.

"You must be joking," said Bella, turning towards the mountains. "I'm going after my father." The Quetzal slapped his forehead with his wing.

"Never, ever, does as she's told," he thought incredulously, flying after her at full pelt. "I can play some tricks with Greenwich meantime," he panted, "but pretty soon your mum's going to find out you're no longer in the attic. Try explaining that after nine o'clock on a Friday night."

Bella didn't need the Quetzal to guide her. With all the speed she could muster she was soon flying above the peaks of the Simian Mountains.

Looking down through the white clouds at the deep gorges and interlocking valleys, Bella wondered how she had ever managed to cross it so quickly by foot.

"I really can do anything I set my mind to," she told herself, feeling her confidence return. Her sense of purpose was also clear. "I'm never, ever going to stop looking for my father. We will be together. I know we will."

For the Quetzal, the flight across the Simian Mountains was bringing nothing but stress.

"Have you forgotten what the plumage of a quetzal looks like to a raptor?" he wheezed, trying his best to keep up. "It's like a red rag to a bull, that's what it is." But there was no stopping Bella once her mind was set. Luckily, with the sun already setting, the silhouette of two quetzals flying at great speed over the mountains was observed by only a handful of owls who were wise enough to keep their beaks shut. For now, anyway, many of the predatory birds were more preoccupied with sleeping after the battle than chasing snacks.

The two travellers journeyed for almost an hour before the low mist hanging over the crater came into view.

"Are you sure you want to be doing this?" asked the Quetzal, nervously, as they approached the rim.

To Bella's distress and the Quetzal's relief, the crater was empty but for the ravaged carcasses of Karpov's pre-battle feast. The stench was awful.

"Where have they all gone?" Bella asked clasping her hand over her nose.

"They've disbanded," the quetzal replied as soon as he could catch his breath.

"But how will I find my father now?" Bella pleaded.

The Quetzal was feeling dizzy. "I'm too old for this," he was thinking.

"I guess it depends whether or not he wants to be found," he replied sounding jaded.

Bella felt very confused. The notion that her father may have chosen to disappear was too upsetting to contemplate.

"Of course he wants to be found," she insisted.

Bella sat on the floor of the crater and buried her head into her hands. "This is a nightmare," she thought, wondering if she would ever see her father again. "I've come all this way to meet my father and I still don't understand any of the things that really matter to me."

The Quetzal, who was becoming much more skilled in dealing with his human twin than Bella acknowledged, left her alone for a few moments and went to perch on a nearby rock.

"Did I overhear you telling your father that you have friends in Lalibela?" he asked finally.

The Quetzal's words seemed to hang in the air until Bella eventually registered them. When she did, the thought of seeing Yohanis and Mahlet was exciting.

"The Corporation were trying to take control of their cooperative," Bella told the Quetzal, raising her head.

"Well, let's see how they got on," said the Quetzal, opening his wings.

As they glided down towards Lalibela, Bella saw the Balai herding his goats along the mountain path.

"Thanks again for all your help," she called after him. The old man looked up but didn't reply.

Even with her eyes closed, the warm, comforting aroma of coffee beans would have led Bella back. She landed close to an olive tree on the outskirts of town.

"Not you again," snorted the donkey tethered to the tree.

"Donkey!" Bella cheered, running over to give him a pat on the back. Since her hasty exist from the Balai's cave, Bella had been so busy she'd forgotten all about him.

"Before you ask – don't!" warned the donkey. "Whatever

it is, I'm not up for it. I've been lugging sacks of coffee around all day and I'm beat!"

Bella gathered up an armful of the lush grass that grew outside the donkey's range and laid it down before him.

"I'm hungry too, you know," shrieked the Quetzal from his perch in the tree.

Bella was soon running through the town calling for her friends.

"Mahlet! Yohanis!"

All around, the smiles and waves Bella attracted reminded her how friendly the Ethiopian people had been throughout this trip.

By now, most families were making their final preparations for dinner.

"Take the next right," called a girl Bella recognized from the football match they'd played in the town square.

It didn't take her long to locate the neighbourhood she was looking for. To her delight, she found her two friends sitting with their mother by a small fire outside their house. What struck Bella immediately was that their mother was no longer wearing black, but a lovely, white cotton dress instead.

"There's Bella!" cried Mahlet, jumping up to greet her friend.

"We were all talking about you," said Yohanis, offering Bella his hand.

"Sit down and let me bring you some food," said Mrs Alemnew kindly.

"No," said another voice, from inside the house. "Let me bring it."

Bella looked at the door. She recognized the voice but hesitated for fear her ears were deceiving her.

"Mr Alemnew?" she called doubtfully.

The children's father emerged from the house on his crutches carrying a plateful of food.

"He looks so confident and proud," thought Bella, shocked by his transformation.

"I'll get some water and make some fresh coffee," said Mahlet, running to the well.

Instead of his old army uniform, Mr Alemnew was wearing the familiar sackcloth robes worn by so many in his community.

"It's good to see you, Bella," he smiled. "We prayed that you might come."

It wasn't long before Bella and the Quetzal were eating and listening to the story of Mr Alemnew's triumphant return.

". . . We were literally about to sign the contract with the Corporation," said Yohanis, picking up from where his sister had left off. "Mr Letellier was there with his pen and a briefcase full of American dollars when my father walked in through the door."

"It was a miracle," said Mahlet as she scattered incense onto the fire. "Father practically kicked Mr Letellier out of the village."

Yohanis gave her a poke in the ribs for her insensitive turn of phrase but Mr Alemnew was quick to reassure.

"My family was so brave," he told Bella. "If it wasn't for their stirring speeches the night before, the whole deal would have already been signed."

"But no one crosses my father," said Mahlet proudly. "Next week, we're meeting representatives from fair trade companies based in Britain and America."

"But that's wonderful!" said Bella. "You stood up for something that you believe in and you won – even against the Corporation!"

The idea that her father's battle against the Corporation could be waged on small battlefronts like this all over the world and be so successful filled Bella with optimism. She started to understand what her father had tried to explain to her about the wider battle. "If every individual we speak to at the meeting goes back home and does something for our cause – even in the tiniest of ways," he'd said, "the word will spread. If this happens in enough places, Karpov and the Corporation will ultimately fail." Mr Alemnew put his hand on Bella's shoulder.

"I told everyone about you," he said gently. "Imagine my surprise when they could describe exactly how you looked." He gave Bella a kind, quizzical look that made her feel a little awkward. "Perhaps I should have been more truthful and straightforward with Mr Alemnew when I met him," she thought.

"What news do you have of your father?" asked Mahlet keenly.

"And Guereza," Yohanis added. "I knew he'd go after you, the little monkey."

Bella considered how accepting Yohanis and Mahlet had been about the fact that she could transform herself into a quetzal and speak to animals.

"It's as if they instinctively understand our connection with nature," she thought, wishing more people back home felt the same way.

While Bella had never felt entirely at ease with the way Yohanis and Mahlet sometimes kept Guereza tethered like a pet, Guereza himself had never complained to her about the way he'd been treated.

As a small gathering of neighbours joined the Alemnew family under a glorious starry sky to hear Bella's story, the sleepy Quetzal slipped away. Sometimes, Bella found her tale difficult to tell and would have to stop for a drink to help steady her emotions, especially as the story reached its depressing climax with Karpov and the rakah. She contemplated not telling Mahlet and Yohanis about the Guereza's heroic death, but then decided that to leave them with the false hope of his return would be cruel. When she was done, Mahlet put her arms around Bella and gave her a hug.

"You're very brave, Bella," she told her. Yohanis put some more charcoal onto the fire.

"Thank you for all the things you said to Guereza at the end," he said. "I think you were both heroes." But Bella didn't feel like a hero at all. Telling the part about her father's dramatic exit with the rakah made her feel ashamed. She could think of no plausible reason why he would have deserted her so willingly.

"I'll go and make up a bed for our guest," said Mrs Alemnew, collecting the empty cups. Bella was relieved. The thought of travelling home without a good night's sleep was too much. She looked up into the tree to see how the Quetzal was bearing up and found that he was already snoring.

The Alemnews' neighbours began to return to their homes, full of the wonder of Bella's story. Mr Alemnew sent his children on after their mother to help prepare the room for their guest and waited for his moment. Bella had the impression he had something he wanted to say to her in private.

"Our country once had a great leader called Haile Selassie," he started. He wet his lips with the last of his coffee and threw the dregs onto the fire. "He said that throughout history, it was the inaction and indifference of people who should have known better, and the silence of the voice of justice when it mattered most, that made it possible for evil to triumph."

"That's what people are like sometimes," said Bella. "I'm always telling people to speak out – otherwise things only get worse."

Mr Alemnew nodded thoughtfully.

"From what you have told us," he said, "you sound very much like your father." He paused for a moment, giving the impression that he wasn't entirely sure he ought to share his thoughts. "But what makes me sad, Bella, is that you sound so angry with him. Like he's betrayed you in some way."

Bella felt her body tense. Mr Alemnew's words were uncomfortably close to the truth. Unsure of what to say, she simply shrugged her shoulders and stared into the fire.

"My father's been kidnapped by the enemy," she said quietly. "For all I know, he's dead."

They sat in silence for a while longer, listening to the sound of crackling charcoal.

"I have a secret that I would like to share with you," said Mr Alemnew. He gave the fire a poke with a stick and looked around to make sure no one was listening. "You must promise me that you will never say a word of this to anyone." The urgency of his tone sharpened Bella's senses. She looked him straight in the eye.

"I don't like secrets," she told him. "Before I came on this journey I kept a secret from my best friend and now she hates me."

Mr Alemnew looked thoughtful. "I know you'll do the right thing, Bella," he told her. "I trust you." He collected his thoughts by staring into the dying embers of the fire.

"During the war I was ordered on a secret mission to gather information on our enemy's weaponry," he began.

"Bella, your bed's ready," called Mahlet bursting out through the door and running towards them.

Bella glanced into Mr Alemnew's watery eyes.

"Anyway," said Mr Alemnew hurriedly, his story barely started. "All I really wanted to say was – don't give up on your father. Trust that he loves you and keep an open mind."

"Come on," said Mahlet, taking Bella's hand. "Let me show you where to wash."

"But why would he go off with the rakah so willingly?" she wanted to ask Mr Alemnew. "And why are you telling me about a secret mission?"

But the moment was gone.

CHAPTER TWENTY-THREE

LONDON

Bella woke up early the next morning. She tiptoed around the sleeping bodies and out through the door. With the sun yet to rise above the mountains, the air was blissfully cool and Bella decided to make her way down to the well for a drink. As she cut a pathway through the wandering chickens and goats and looked out across the mountains, she tried to imagine herself by her father's side. She stopped for a moment and closed her eyes. "Where are you, Father?" she whispered. So many times in the past, Bella had met her father in her dreams in places that she now knew to be real. "Maybe we do have the power to be connected wherever we are," she thought. She tried to conjure up her father's image, but all she could see was darkness. Feeling dispirited, she carried on.

"Selam," said Bella, finding Yohanis at the well filling his buckets.

"Selam," he replied.

Bella could tell that her friend had been deep in thought and felt a little uncomfortable that she'd interrupted him.

"Here," said Yohanis, "let me pour you some water."

Bella cupped her hands and Yohanis poured.

"Please don't think I'm rude," Yohanis began as Bella drank and washed her face. "But last night, when we all went in, did my father tell you about what really happened to him during the war?" Bella had to stop and think. Mr Alemnew had wanted to tell her some secret but there hadn't been enough time.

"He told me to have faith in my father," she told Yohanis. Bella could see that her friend was deeply puzzled.

"And nothing about what happened to himself?" Yohanis urged. Bella couldn't think of anything else.

"I think he wanted to tell me more, but there wasn't any time," she told him. "But surely he's told you everything." Bella could tell by the confused look on Yohanis' face that he was unsure.

"I don't think that he has," said Yohanis shakily. "I think he's too proud to say but I think maybe he was a spy and when they found out . . ." Yohanis was looking tearful. "I was thinking of how Karpov must have tortured Guereza and wondering how my father really lost his legs." Bella put her arm around her friend and stood in silence with him for some time. "War is such an awful, awful thing," she was thinking. "How can anyone think it's heroic to kill or maim a fellow living creature?"

"I'm sure your father will tell you everything in time," she reassured him. "For now, all you can do is keep an open mind and trust that he loves you." They returned to the house where Mrs Alemnew was preparing breakfast.

Bella had quite a bit of experience saying goodbye to friends in foreign places. It didn't make this farewell any easier. After they'd all eaten, they went outside.

"Please say whatever you have to say quickly," said the Quetzal as he perched on Bella's shoulder, nibbling at a sizeable piece of injera. "I hate a long goodbye."

"Good luck with the cooperative," Bella told the Alemnew family as they and quite a number of their neighbours gathered around her. "I'll keep a lookout for your coffee in the supermarket."

"Perhaps you could set up a market stall and sell some for us," Mahlet suggested. The idea seemed a little farfetched to Bella at the time but she promised to give it some thought.

"We all pray that you find your father again soon," Yohanis added. Bella was touched, but in her heart she was starting to feel that she would never see her father again.

"You fell from the sky the day you arrived," Yohanis reminded her. "One minute you were like that bird on your shoulder, the next . . ." He was searching for the right thing to say. ". . . you were just you. Are you sure you're not an angel?" Despite her sadness, Bella couldn't help but smile.

"If my mum could hear you ask that question she'd be in hysterics," she told them. "I'm always in far too much trouble for anyone to call me an angel back home." Thinking of her adoptive mum made Bella feel calm. "I can't wait to see her," she thought. "At least she's always been there for me."

As she made her final farewells and transformed herself into her animal twin right before them, Bella was again touched by how easy it was to be herself with people she trusted in foreign lands. "I really wish I could tell Charlie and my mum about all this," she thought. "Maybe I will."

Bella and the Quetzal flew up and away from the Ethiopian highlands and northwards, following the trail of the Blue Nile up into Egypt.

"This was the route the Knights Templar took to smuggle

the Ark of the Covenant into Ethiopia," she called to the Quetzal as they flew over the coach-loads of tourists making their way towards the Valley of the Kings and the great temples at Karnak.

"Don't tell me you believe in any of that Knights Templar rubbish?" snapped the Quetzal, testily. "There are more prophesies about those knights and that chest than there are about you."

"Well that's good to know," replied Bella. "Because quite frankly, I'd be happy if I never heard one of those stories ever again!"

Travelling home with the Quetzal as her guide felt much quicker to Bella than the outward journey.

"So how do you play so many tricks with time?" Bella asked her trusty friend, recalling her own useless tamperings with the clocks at school.

"I suppose you might work it out," said the Quetzal rather snottily. "Eventually."

Bella chose not to get into a row. The Quetzal had been such a great companion on her adventures so far she didn't know what she would do without him. By the time they found themselves choking their way through the polluted London sky, the moon and stars were already twinkling above them.

"Am I late for dinner?" asked Bella fretfully.

"It's touch and go," said the Quetzal. "Your mum's already climbing the ladder to the attic, wondering where you are."

Bella swooped down onto the roof of 14 Birdcage Crescent and made to lower herself back through the skylight.

"Bella Balistica, what are you doing?" cried Annie, poking her head up into the attic to see her daughter scrambling in from the roof.

"I . . . I . . ." Bella stammered, happy beyond words to be reunited with her mum but with absolutely no idea how she was going to explain herself.

"I'm going to have that skylight sealed up," said Annie, as distressed as she was cross to think that her daughter could have fallen to her death. "And what happened to your plaster and sling?" Annie's eyes shot down to the broken pieces of plaster on the floor.

"My arm's fine," Bella pleaded as she watched her mum lean up over the old Guatemalan chest and bang the skylight shut.

Annie's eyes were trying to take in her daughter's dishevelled appearance.

"Bella, your brand-new trainers!" Annie was about to launch into a full-on investigation when a there was a loud, pitiable squeak from outside.

"There's a bird . . . in distress . . . on the roof," Bella stuttered. "That's why I was up there."

They looked up to the skylight where a forlorn looking Quetzal dropped with a thud onto the glass. The profile of his flattened face looking so miserable and forlorn made Bella and her mum both rush to help him down. Opening the skylight carefully so as not to jettison the bird over the gutter to the patio below, Annie gently wrapped her hands around him and brought him in.

"Oh, Bella," she whispered softly. "Unless I'm very much mistaken, this is a quetzal bird. I saw many of these on my travels in Guatemala. The poor thing has probably been picked on by that vicious falcon I've seen hanging around here such a lot recently."

"Food," whimpered the Quetzal, for Bella's ears. Even without the gift of bird-talk, Annie understood.

"Quick, Bella, go and get a bowl of water and some peanuts from the kitchen."

"And a chocolate biscuit if you have one," chirped the Quetzal, looking remarkably at home in the palm of Annie's hands.

"But don't run down the stairs," Annie added, sitting down on the chest to stroke the Quetzal's back.

"He saved my skin there," thought Bella as she sprinted downstairs. "Only, if he expects me to wait on him hand on foot he's got another . . ."

"I asked you to walk, Bella," called Annie. "Don't you listen to anything I say?"

"I know," Bella heard the Quetzal twitter. "It's like talking to a headstrong mule."

When Bella got back, she could tell that her mum was feeling more upset than cross.

"Bella," she began, as Bella lay down the bowl of water and scattered the peanuts out for the Quetzal. "Don't you think it's a bit strange that this bird managed to find his way to our house?"

"She's off on one," chirped the Quetzal. "Please, I beg you; don't get into one of those horrible mushy conversations you humans . . ."

"Quit moaning, for goodness sake," Bella chirped to the Quetzal. The second the words left her lips Bella knew she'd slipped up.

"Bella!" gasped Annie. "You were twittering like a bird." Bella was distraught with embarrassment.

"I was only mimicking him," she stuttered, "I . . ."

"You sounded exactly like him, Bella," Annie insisted with tears in her eyes. "The day I met your mother in that orphanage in Quetzaltenango, the very day on which you were born, she was twittering away exactly as you were then with a quetzal who looked remarkably like this bird!"

"You see," chirped the Quetzal dismissively. "Exactly what I was talking about."

Bella had been desperate to tell her mum everything for months.

"Mum," she said, getting excited. "Over the last year or so . . ."

"No!" squealed the Quetzal. "Don't do it. She'll never understand."

"Keep out of this," Bella warned the Quetzal. "This is something I need to do."

"Ah!" Annie exclaimed, clasping her hands to her face. "You're doing it again!"

Bella took one look at the disbelief in her mum's eyes and thought better of it. Luckily for everyone, the phone was ringing.

"I'll get it," said Bella, scrambling down the ladder. But by the time she got to the phone it had stopped. She quickly dialled the code to get the incoming number. It was Charlie's.

"Who was it?" asked her mum, carefully climbing down the stairs with the Quetzal.

"I missed it," said Bella. "I think it was the bank."

"Oh, those people," Annie grumbled. "Probably on to us to take out a loan we've absolutely no interest in."

Annie set the Quetzal up in a little box that she lined with cotton wool and placed him in the conservatory looking out onto the garden.

"You couldn't turn me around and put the telly on, could you?" he asked Bella when Annie left.

"No, I could not!" chirped Bella. "We don't have the telly on while we're eating." Bella was relieved that the Quetzal hadn't rushed off, but it was a bit weird having him in the house.

As Bella and Annie sat down to dinner, the phone rang again.

"Probably the bank again," said Bella, knowing her mum never picked up the phone while they were eating.

"My guess is that it's Charlie," said Annie. "I'm sure she's as upset as you are that you've had this falling out. Do you want to tell me what happened?"

One of Annie's exceptional qualities as a parent was that she never pressed Bella on anything, knowing full well that Bella would come and tell her things when she was ready. Tonight, however, Annie was too stirred up by all that was going on.

". . . so this boy, Mickey, grabbed and snogged you without any warning?" she started off, trying to stay calm as she poured chilli con carne over their jacket potatoes. Inside, she was thinking: "Please don't tell me this is the start of all that fancying boys thing. It's far too early for that."

"He's such a slime-ball," said Bella, tucking into her dinner with relish. "He knows Charlie really likes him and he hardly gives her the time of day."

Bella too was glad the conversation had been diverted away from her apparent ability to converse with her mother's favourite quetzal.

"Well, I think he was out of order," said Annie, gazing with astonishment at Bella's arm and deciding that it couldn't have been broken at all. "And I think you should tell Charlie exactly what happened."

After dinner, Annie switched the kettle on to make herself a pot of coffee and was surprised when Bella asked if she could have a small cup too.

"I didn't think you liked coffee," said Annie.

"Where does this coffee come from?" asked Bella as the smell from the cafetiére drifted in from the kitchen.

"It's Ethiopian fair trade," said Annie. "Why?"

"I only wondered," said Bella. She was thinking about what Mahlet had said to her as she was leaving Lalibela and added: "Hey Mum, you know how we're always searching the supermarket for fair trade products?"

"Yeah . . .?" said Annie cautiously.

"Well, what about if we got a stall in the Sunday market at Greenwich and sold only fair trade products?" Bella could tell by the wide-eyed expression on her mum's face that she'd stumbled upon something that interested her greatly. "We could sell handicrafts made by the street children we met in India." Bella was getting excited. "And Guatemalan fair trade chocolate!" she cheered, licking her lips.

"You know, Bella, I've thinking about suggesting such a thing myself," said Annie.

"And I think we should try and make links with new cooperatives like the ones I was reading about on the internet in the highlands of Ethiopia – and see if we can sell their coffee," Bella continued, hardly letting her mum get a word in edgewise. "And then, any money we raise for ourselves we can donate to the children's charities we already campaign for."

"Can't you keep the noise down?" squawked the Quetzal from his cozy little box. "I'm trying to get some sleep here!"

That night, Bella waited to hear her mum's snores before she tiptoed back up to the attic to speak to the portrait.

"I'm sorry, Mother," said Bella, standing before her father's painting. "I lost the pendant." She waited for the voice to speak to her inside her head like it always did, but nothing came. "And I think my father's dead."

It was the first time Bella had admitted this to herself since the rakah had whisked him away from the summit. She closed her eyes and replayed the memory of his departing words: "Harak, karadak, lopatos, almanos. Love, learn, forgive and move on."

"I love you, Father," she sobbed as she climbed into the hammock. As for the 'moving on', Bella had absolutely no idea where to start.

CHAPTER TWENTY-FOUR

PICKING UP THE PIECES

The next day was Saturday. Bella got up early and went down to check on the Quetzal but he was nowhere to be found.

"He must be somewhere," yawned Annie, descending the stairs in her dressing gown. "I shut every window in the house."

The gentle swinging of the cat-flap alerted them to the re-emergence of their notoriously wild cat.

"Prudence," Annie reproached. "What have you done with the quetzal?"

Bella and her mum stood rooted to the spot and for a moment Bella had the strangest sense that her mum was actually expecting Prudence to answer in a way that she would understand.

"The pompous old wind-bag pecked my ear and flew off," Prudence meowed bitterly for Bella's ears only. "And good riddance to him, that's what I say." Bella could tell by the cut on Prudence's ear that for once she was telling the truth.

"The Quetzal will be alright," Bella reassured her mum. "I'm sure he'll be back."

Bella hadn't been picked for the football team because of her injured arm, so she and her mum took the bus into Greenwich. They made enquiries about market stalls at Bella's favourite shop, The Quetzal, which sold fair trade clothing and nick-nacks made in Guatemala.

"Are you alright, Bella?" asked Annie. "You seem a bit down today." Annie was thinking Bella's sadness was related to the conversation they'd started yesterday about the Quetzal and her birthmother.

"I'm okay," said Bella. "I was only thinking about my father."

"Oh," said Annie, kindly. It was unusual for Bella to reply so naturally to a comment about her mood. "Well, is it anything you want to ta–"

"I don't," Bella interrupted. Then, giving her mum a smile. "But thanks, Mum."

After they'd picked up the forms from the shop, they were walking around the square to find a café when Bella spotted a brochure for Turkey in the window of the travel agent.

"I didn't know you were interested in Turkey," said Annie, following Bella's gaze. "Perhaps we should pick up some brochures. We need to start thinking about booking something for next summer."

As usual, they emerged with a pile of magazines featuring holiday destinations all over the world.

"I'm so happy you like to explore new places," Annie told Bella. "And it's great you like football and fencing more than you like boys." Bella pulled a face at the mere mention of 'boys' but inside she knew she hadn't told her mum the complete story.

"I could have stopped Mickey from kissing me," she thought guiltily. "Only something about it was exciting and I wanted to know what it felt like." She didn't say this to her mum, though.

As they sat in the café, Bella began to browse through the

Turkey brochures. It wasn't long before she found a hotel not too far from the Nemrud Mountain she'd heard the pelican speak about at the summit meeting – the place where the Corporation were believed to be setting up their new headquarters. She read about the Adiyaman province in which Nemrud stood and was astonished to learn that historians believed it to be the very cradle of civilization itself. She tried to imagine what secrets the burial chamber of Antiochus I held and the awesome powers that might be contained within the magnificent statues of the gods that guarded it.

"Now what was that place that pelican at the summit was talking about?" thought Bella, racking her brains. "Something about a forgotten kingdom."

"Nemrud," Annie keenly observed, looking over Bella's shoulder. "Isn't that where Ted Briggs has recently been on his archaeological digs?" Bella was dumfounded. It was the first she'd heard about Briggs' trip. "He's bound to be caught up in all this somewhere," she thought.

Bella wanted to get a book about the Knights Templar and when they couldn't find one in the Greenwich bookshop they made their way to the library.

"We haven't got any in at the moment," said the librarian, scrolling down a list of titles on her monitor. "But we can order any of these for you if you fill out a form." Annie was used to Bella's interest in all kinds of 'boys own' topics.

"I suppose you're interested in the swords and weapons," she offered as Bella examined the list.

"Kind of," said Bella.

Bella's eye was drawn to a book called Meleya.

"I'll order that one," said Bella, pointing to it on the

screen. The librarian clicked onto the internal link for more information.

"That's an ancient manuscript thought to have been written by the Knights Templar themselves," she told Bella, shaking her head sadly. "I'm afraid you need to make an appointment at the British Museum in London to read that one."

"We can do that," said Annie excitedly. "I've been meaning to catch up with Jim Green for months. Let's do it. I'll give him a ring."

Bella was delighted. She liked Jim. Annie had met him in Australia on one of her backpacking trips and had always kept in touch. He was eccentric and was absolutely mad about football. Bella and Annie always had a fun time when they hooked up with him.

Later that afternoon, Bella went up to the small room her mum had once used for developing film before she switched to digital cameras. Now that it was an office, Bella spent quite a bit of time here. She was logging on to the internet to find out more about Nemrud and the Forgotten Kingdom when there was a knock at the door. Her mum answered.

"Bella, it's Charlie," called Annie.

Bella bounded down the stairs to find Charlie at the door with her ice skates hanging over her shoulder. Bella could tell at once that she was upset.

"Charlie, I'm so sorry about the other day," Bella began.

"Bella, why don't you invite Charlie up to the attic and I'll bring up some juice and cake," Annie suggested.

"Thank you, Mrs Balistica," said Charlie meekly. "Is that alright, Bella? I'd like to come up."

Bella was really happy to see Charlie but was a little

apprehensive about the conversation they were sure to have. They went straight to the attic.

"Bella," said Charlie, putting down her skates and taking a seat on the Guatemalan chest. "I've got something to tell you." Bella could tell she was feeling embarrassed because she kept her eyes to the ground and fiddled with her hair. "The second I put the phone down to you yesterday, I had a text from Mickey inviting me to go ice-skating today."

"That's great, Charlie," said Bella, sitting down on the floor. "That's what you wanted, right?" Charlie looked up.

"Oh, Bella, you're so lovely," she said kindly. "But I didn't know what I should do. I mean, I knew you must like him too and that he liked you – anyone can see that. But I've never had a boyfriend before and I couldn't help myself." Charlie looked mortified.

"Hey," Bella whispered gently, putting a hand on Charlie's arm. "It's okay." But Charlie was shaking.

"Anyway," Charlie blurted, desperate to get everything out into the open. "We went skating this morning and I kissed him."

Bella hated to see Charlie so distressed and wanted to ease her conscience quickly.

"Charlie, you're easily the prettiest Year Seven girl in the school. If you want to go out with Mickey, that's fine with me," said Bella. "I'm not ready to have a boyfriend – not for ages. I much prefer hanging out with you." Charlie's eyes were starting to well up.

"You're my best friend, Bella," she sobbed. "And Mickey's a pig." Bella was shocked. Charlie always said nice things about everyone. "Do you know, his real name is Michel?" Charlie continued. "And just because his father is some hot-shot French businessman and he thinks he has the physique of a god, he thinks that he can get away with anything he wants. Well I tell you, Bella, he can't – at least, not with me."

"Why?" asked Bella. "What happened?"

Charlie looked mortified. "We'd only been skating for two minutes when he grabbed me and started to kiss me," she garbled. "I was a bit scared at first and then I started to kiss him back." Charlie was sobbing. "I couldn't help myself." Bella knew exactly what Charlie meant. "And then he started in on you," Charlie went on. "Telling me all these things about you and your family that really upset me."

"Like what?" asked Bella. "He doesn't know the first thing about me."

"He said you were a liar and a thief. That you broke into Ted Briggs' pet shop last Christmas, released all his animals and stole valuable artefacts from his private collection."

"That's not true!" Bella cried, more in response to the latter charge than the first.

"He said you told lies to the Indian police about Mr Briggs' involvement with children working in Indian sweatshops to get him arrested and have his sports shop closed down."

"Charlie, it was all true – ask my mum," Bella pleaded. "It all happened when we were on holiday last summer."

"It gets worse," said Charlie, feeling less sure about going on. "He told me that you have secrets." She stopped and looked Bella in the eye. "I told him he was a liar. That you and I were best friends. That there were no secrets between us. That's right, isn't it, Bella?" she asked nervously.

"That's right," Bella quivered. Bella didn't feel on solid ground now at all. There were so many things she kept from her dear friend she hardly knew where to start.

"He told me that you go out on your own late at night, getting up to all kind of things." They heard the sound of footsteps on the ladder.

"Banana cake and apple juice," said Annie merrily, laying the tray on the floor and sliding it along to Bella. "And I don't know what that boy Mickey what's-his-name is on about. Unless Bella has the power to float over our alarm lasers on the stairs and in the hall – or better still, fly out the house through the skylight – I can personally vouch for the fact that she's in bed by nine every night of the week. It's a house rule – unless, of course, she stays up to watch football with me."

Bella had half a mind to fly off the handle at her mum's participation in a very personal conversation. Luckily, though, her mum had only picked up on a fragment of it and what she had to say had come as a blessing.

"I know, Mrs Balistica," said Charlie. "He's such a liar!" Annie made a discreet withdrawal.

It wasn't long before Charlie and Bella were swinging happily together in the hammock, chatting about how much they hated boys and how silly the older girls were to be so hung up on them. They scoffed their cake, drank their juice and at five o'clock Bella put on the radio to hear the football scores. Charlie's mum had arrived to pick Charlie up, when suddenly Charlie remembered something.

"Oh, Bella, I've got to tell you this – it's so freaky!" she said, getting up to go. "As I was snogging Mickey, I happened to pull on his jumper and saw the tattoo on the top of his shoulder." Bella was laughing, completely unprepared for what was about to come.

"Don't tell me," she giggled. "Cupid. Michel's got a tattoo of a mythical love angel."

"No," Charlie sniggered, "but you're on the right track. Michel Letellier has a tattoo of a hideous harpy-like creature – only his beast has the armoured head of a medieval knight."

CHAPTER TWENTY-FIVE

BOLT FROM THE BLUE

Hearing Mickey's surname for the first time and discovering that he had a tattoo of a rakah on his shoulder was a shock to Bella.

"Michel Letellier," she was thinking, "How come I never got to hear his full name before?"

How she managed to hold herself together to say goodbye to Charlie was a miracle.

"So all this time the Corporation have had their spies watching me," Bella sobbed to the portrait of her mother as soon as Charlie had gone. "Why couldn't I see what was going on?"

Bella had no doubt that Mickey was the 'little spy' Askar Karpov had referred to during their sword fight in Bahir Dar.

"And that man with the briefcase in Lalibela," Bella continued. "That's Mickey's dad." But still the portrait was quiet. "What's going on?" Bella begged.

First thing Monday morning when Bella got to school, she was reminded that she had five straight detentions.

"Mrs Briggs called the headteacher to say you were trespassing on railway property in your school uniform," Mr Appleby told her as he announced Bella's punishment before the whole form group. But that wasn't the worst of it. Eugene Briggs was finding his feet rapidly amongst the school bullies. Not surprisingly, Michel Letellier was suddenly no longer available for flirtatious chats; quite the contrary, it was Mickey who was leading the assault. Text messages and rumours about Charlie and Bella started to spread like wildfire.

"Imogen Meeks says she's heard girls saying that we're both boy haters. That we lead boys on, snog them and then blank them out," Charlie told Bella at the first break Monday morning.

Not only was there constant heckling from Eugene and Mickey, but Bella and Charlie were ostracized from almost every social clique.

"We're on our own," Charlie told Bella as she walked her down to her detention that afternoon. "What are we going to do?"

Charlie was receiving so many threats on her mobile phone she'd decided to switch it off and leave it at home for the rest of the week. She felt so nervous about walking home on her own, she waited for Bella to finish her detentions. The only thing all week to distract Bella from her own misery was the arrival of a new boy called Harvey Stills. It was obvious right from the moment he limped into the room that Harvey was going to be a target for Eugene Briggs.

"Look at his twisted foot," Bella heard Eugene hiss to Connor Mitchell. "He's a cripple."

"What have you heard about him?" Bella heard Charlie ask Imogen Meeks in the cloakrooms later that day.

"Apparently, this is his fifth school in three years," she told Charlie. It was when Bella saw Harvey standing alone in the school playground that her interest flared.

"He looks so scared," she said to Charlie.

"He certainly looks miserable," replied Charlie.

"I reckon he's been bullied badly at one of his other schools," said Bella. "I think we need to look out for him."

The headline news on Tuesday was totally depressing. The announcement from the G8 summit in New York was that there was no agreement on issues relating to global warming and fair trade.

"And these people are running the world," Annie complained in disgust as she and Bella sat on the sofa following the report. "Half the reason the developing world is so poor is because of us. If we paid them a fair price for what they sold us, the world would be a much better place."

The whole feature was totally depressing. But things were set to get worse still.

The next Saturday, both the girls' and boys' football teams were playing at home. Bella had managed to get a medical note from a very confused doctor at the local clinic that her arm was perfectly fine, and she'd managed to get herself back into the side. Annie had decided to spend the day organizing things for their market stall so Bella got a lift with Charlie's mum.

Everything about the day started out typically. Mrs Stevens dropped them off on her way to the hair salon.

"Okay girls, have a good match," she smiled, craning her head around to bid them farewell. "You'll be fine to walk home afterwards, won't you?"

"Yes, Mum," said Charlie, getting out of the car.

"Thanks, Mrs Stevens," said Bella.

Arriving so close to kick-off time, the girls found that the grounds were already full of players and spectators. Bella and Charlie were already in their kits and were soon making their way towards the pitch to meet up with Mr Appleby.

"Pig-face!" someone shouted.

Expecting to see Eugene Briggs, Bella turned around ready to give him a piece of her mind, when she realized that Eugene wasn't alone.

"Ted Briggs," Bella gasped at the sight of the tall man in the shabby khaki suit.

"Bella Balistica," Professor Briggs grinned slyly, doffing his white safari hat in a parody of a respect. "A pleasure, as always." Bella withered at the sight of Briggs' yellowing teeth and dark, menacing eyes.

"Let me introduce you to an old friend of mine," said Briggs, turning to the strikingly handsome man in the black suit to his right. Even if the young Mickey Letellier hadn't been alongside him, Bella would have known instantly who the man was.

"That must be Mickey's dad," Charlie whispered. The two men and their offspring moved discreetly towards their prey.

"You need to stop your son from calling people names," Bella told Mr Briggs. "He's not going to get away with his pathetic bullying antics at this school!"

Up-close, the stale whiff of Briggs' sweat and tobacco made Bella gag.

"So this is the infamous girl everyone talks about," said Mr Letellier in a thick French accent. His crystal blue eyes cut Bella an icy stare. "Haven't we met before somewhere?" he asked snidely.

"And where would that be?" Bella challenged.

"Mr Letellier flew in from New York this morning," Ted Briggs interjected.

"A funeral for an old friend," Letellier smiled as he ran his fingers through his blond hair.

"I wonder whose funeral that could have been," thought Bella, her mind shooting to straight to Askar Karpov.

"Which is where, incidentally, I had a very interesting conversation about you," Mr Letellier concluded wryly.

"Okay girls, huddle up!" called Mr Appleby, his voice booming around the fields.

"Come on, Dad," said Mickey. "If you want to see a good game you'd better come with me and Eugene. The girls' team is the worst!"

"Bye, pig-face," sneered Eugene as they turned to leave.

Bella didn't bother to reply. She'd moved on from tit-for-tat retaliations with morons like Eugene Briggs. What was of concern to her was Mickey's dad's comment that he'd been having conversations about her in New York last week.

"What do you make of that 'conversations' thing Mr Letellier was on about?" asked Charlie as they ran to join up with their teammates.

"Ah, it's nothing," Bella groaned. "Mickey probably put him up to it to spook me out."

"Well, given that he was dressed for a funeral, he did a pretty good job," said Charlie. "At least with me."

Bella found it hard to concentrate on the game. She wanted to know for sure whose funeral Mr Letellier had been attending and with whom he might have been talking there. With Briggs and Letellier always in view as they followed the boy's match on the next pitch, Bella was easily distracted.

"Hey, Bella, isn't that your mum?" Charlie panted, pointing to the parallel touchline as the final whistle blew. To Bella's distress, her mum was finishing up a conversation with Mr Letellier. By the time Bella got there, Letellier was walking away.

"Hey, Bella," smiled Annie. "I managed to organize the suppliers so I called Charlie's mum to say I'd pick you guys up. How did you get on?"

"What were you doing talking to that man?" asked Bella crossly, pointing to Mr Letellier as he walked briskly away. Annie gave Bella a weary look.

"Please, Bella," she sighed. "He only called me over to give me his card. Apparently he's got great contacts in the coffee business."

"Well, we're not using them," said Bella flatly. "That's Mickey's dad!" Annie was suddenly very flustered.

"Sorry, Bella," she said. "If I'd have known I would definitely have said something about his son's inappropriate behaviour."

"Well, it's too late!" said Bella, throwing up her arms in disgust.

"Hi, Mrs Balistica," said Charlie, running up to join them.

"Hey, Charlie," said Annie, grateful for the interruption. "Fancy going out to get a pizza?"

Annie took them back to 14 Birdcage for showers before heading into Greenwich for dinner.

"So when's this new market stall of yours going to open?" asked Charlie as they got into Annie's Mini.

"January, hopefully," said Annie. "But there's still quite a lot to do."

"Well, if you need some help, let me know," said Charlie.

"Great," said Annie.

That night, Bella sat in the office and typed 'The Corporation' into a search engine and very quickly came to a report about the funeral of Corporation Director, Askar Karpov. The report didn't go into detail but said that Mr Karpov had died in an abseiling accident in northern Ethiopia. Bella was reading the article so fast she paid little attention to the picture as it slowly downloaded after the text. Karpov's eulogy was exemplary. As an overseas student from Leningrad, Karpov had graduated top of his year at Harvard Business School before becoming an American citizen. By twenty-five, he was the youngest man ever to make the Corporation board. Only this year, he had speculated on land in southeast Turkey, bought it cheaply and struck oil. Bella was about to close the site when she glanced at the picture taken at Karpov's funeral in New York.

"Bella, are you alright?" called Annie, running up the stairs as soon as she heard Bella's scream. "Bella?" Bella's hands were over her face; her eyes wide open. "Bella, what is it?"

CHAPTER TWENTY-SIX

MOVING ON

"What are you looking so miserable about?" asked the Quetzal, when he dropped through the skylight on Sunday morning.

"Where have you been?" Bella demanded, swinging herself up onto the edge of the hammock. "And when were you going to tell me my father was working for the Corporation?" She'd hardly slept last night because she'd felt so devastated. The picture that had finally downloaded from the internet was of her father and Mickey's dad carrying Askar Karpov's coffin. She'd clicked off the site as soon as her mum arrived, but it had been hard work trying to convince her that she was alright.

"Look," said the Quetzal, hopping down onto the beam above Bella's head. "There's no point dwelling on things you can't do anything about. Despite everything you were told, your instincts about your father being alive were right. What are your instincts telling you now?"

Bella stopped to consider them. Her feelings about her father were confused, but the sense of unity she'd felt at the summit meeting in Ethiopia with all those humans and animals coming together to share the same vision for the future of the planet . . . that was too powerful to ignore.

"We can fight," she said. "If Mr Alemnew and his family can defeat the Corporation, then we can at least try to do the same."

Over the next few weeks, Bella found the support of her

mum inspirational. Together they wrote hundreds of e-mails and made calls to fair trade dealers all around the world. Bella e-mailed her friends Shilpa and Randir in India, who were already exporting fair trade handicrafts to outlets in London and San Francisco, to see if they could put her in contact with some local tea cooperatives. Unknown to her mum, she also managed to get a letter through to Antonio and Francesca – the two children that had helped her in Tikal – to see if they knew of any local cocoa cooperatives.

"It feels more real when you deal with local people in other countries so directly," said Annie as she passed Bella her hot chocolate one night approaching Christmas.

Things at school were slowly getting better, too. Bella and Charlie had gone straight to Mr Appleby and made official complaints, logging a whole series of bullying incidents perpetrated by Eugene and Mickey who both had to go on report.

"You see, it does make a difference to speak out," Bella told Harvey Stills while they lined up for French one afternoon. Bella had witnessed Harvey's humiliation at the pool last week when he'd been too terrified of the water even to get in.

"What do you care?" Harvey challenged Bella. He was starting to get into trouble more and more. What began as harmless fidgeting and monkeying about was escalating to direct rudeness to teachers and fellow pupils.

"I care, because I know what bullying does to you," Bella had said.

Bella had no proof that Harvey had ever been bullied for sure, she just sensed it from his introverted manner. That particular chat turned out to be a turning point in their relationship. Since then, Harvey met up with Bella and Charlie most break-times.

It was the week before Christmas when Annie got a phone call from Jim Green at the British Museum, inviting them up for lunch.

"Can Charlie come?" Bella asked her mum. Bella was finding the whole process of sharing some of the things that really mattered to her totally exhilarating.

"Sure," said Annie.

Bella and Charlie had been spending even more time together than usual since the incident with Mickey.

"I think Charlie's really going to find Christmas difficult this year without her dad," Bella told her mum.

"Maybe we should invite Charlie and her mum over for Christmas dinner," Annie suggested.

"Mum, you're great," smiled Bella.

Bella, Annie and Charlie took the train from Greenwich to Charing Cross and walked up Trafalgar Square to see the big Christmas tree and all the lights around the fountain.

"Right," said Annie, getting out her digital camera, "let's have a photo of you girls under the tree."

The square was packed with tourists, many of whom were taking the same photo opportunity. Normally, Bella would have been embarrassed but she was having such a nice time being out with Charlie and her mum that even she was okay about it.

"Bella, what's happened to your pendant?" asked Annie after she'd taken the shot. "I haven't seen you wearing it for weeks."

"It's safely locked away inside my jewellery box," said Bella. "I just don't want to wear it at the moment." Bella was wondering how she was going to break the news to her mum that she no longer had it. Annie had wanted to put the pendant in a safe-deposit box at the bank but Bella had argued her down.

From Trafalgar Square they took a detour through Covent Garden to see the street performers and give Annie a chance to buy Christmas presents for her colleagues at work.

"I love coming up to London at this time of year, don't you?" Bella smiled, admiring the sparkly displays in the shop windows.

"So, what are you hoping to find in this ancient book?" asked Charlie as they bought roast chestnuts from a man dressed as Father Christmas in the main piazza.

"I want to find out more about the codes of honour the Templar Knights followed," said Bella, enjoying the smell of the nuts and the warmth of the bag in her hands.

"But why?" asked Charlie.

"Because there are people today who secretly follow these ancient customs," replied Bella.

"I hate secrets," said Charlie, blowing onto a chestnut. "They always end up hurting somebody."

Annie sent Jim a text as they approached the museum. By the time they reached the main entrance he was there to greet them.

"Hi there," he called, bounding down the front steps and giving Annie a big hug.

"Are you sure your mum doesn't fancy him?" Charlie whispered, noticing how Annie's face lit up the moment she saw him.

"Nah," said Bella. "He's a mate. Anyway, he's too short."

"He's not," Charlie reprimanded. "I think he's handsome."

It wasn't so much that Jim was short, rather the fact Annie was so tall.

"Hi Bella, hi Charlie," said Jim, shaking their hands in turn. Bella wasn't used to seeing Jim in a suit.

"I thought we'd go straight to the archives and dig out this old manuscript for our budding historian here," said Jim with a quick wink to Annie. "Then, I think we need to eat lots of chocolate cake and chips."

"Jim, you are reprehensible," Annie laughed, as she took Jim's arm and followed him up the steps.

"I think she does like him," said Charlie, as she and Bella started to follow.

"You've got a one-track mind, girl," said Bella with a grin.

Jim led them through a bustling lobby and several quiet passages to the big, brightly lit central library.

"This is where we house the main reference collection," said Jim, pointing to the large, concave building standing within the extension. "The book you requested was filed away amongst all the miles of storage space we have beneath the main building. Even I had to put in a request to get access to this book." They started to make their way up the gently spiralling slope to the automated doors. "Hey, and how's your ancient Amharic?" asked Jim. "Meleya is written in one of the oldest calligraphies we have on record."

"Great," said Charlie. "So we're not going to understand a word of it."

Bella was impressed with the privileged passageway Jim could lead them through with a quick flash of his security pass. The main library was breathtaking, with three floors of books and interconnecting stairways as well as spacious reading areas and rooms for quiet study. With a quick nod to one of the librarians, Jim directed them to a small room on the ground floor, smartly furnished with a varnished table and four leather-bound chairs.

"I'm going to have to ask you all to wear these," he told them, pulling white cotton gloves from a dispenser on the wall. "This manuscript is very much one of its kind and you're going to be handling the original."

There was a gentle tap on the door.

"I'll put it out on the table," said the librarian, arriving with a trolley on which rested a large, black book. Bella could see from the spine that the book was damaged.

"I'm afraid some of the pages have been eaten, most probably by rats," said Jim. "But it's still a highly enlightning artefact. Where would you like to start?"

"At the beginning, of course," said Bella.

Bella recognized the calligraphy. She'd seen it in the bible read by the priest outside the church her father had taken her to. Even then, the text had been familiar to her. By the end of the first page, Bella already had a good grasp of the language. While Bella read, Jim was keeping Annie and Charlie engaged with stories and legends surrounding the book.

". . . Some people believe that this book sets in stone all the customs and rituals the Knights Templar introduced into their sect. That way, simply by a certain way of saying things or a particular grip of a handshake, they could tell if someone was part of their wider entourage – a member of their elite business club, if you like."

"So they basically looked after their own," said Annie.

"And pretty much destroyed anyone who wasn't," Jim added.

Bella was reading as quickly as she could. While she couldn't be certain, she hoped that what she discovered here would help her to understand what was happening with her father and the Corporation. She found rituals about all kinds of things – how members were initiated, a complex system of taxes that was traced back to the eight knights of the inner circle, rules about dress, language, business etiquette, and duels. The list was extensive and she was only on page twenty with at least two hundred still to go.

"You actually look like you're reading this book," Charlie commented after a while.

"The text is beautiful to look at even if you don't understand it," said Jim. "Is there anything in particular that you want to know, Bella? I do have some knowledge of the language myself."

"You said that some people believe this book was written by the Templar Knights," said Bella. "But how can you be so sure?" Jim pulled himself up tall.

"An excellent question, Bella," he replied thoughtfully.

"You should hear her in history," said Charlie. "She asks so many questions it drives everyone crazy." Annie and Jim smiled but Bella wanted Jim to cut to the chase.

"I mean, could this book have been written by a group that started out being part of the Knights Templar but then broke away?" she asked.

"Bella, what have you been reading?" asked Annie.

"You're right," said Jim quickly, inspired by Bella's grasp of a theory he also held great store by. "There are many of us who believe the Knights Templar were overwhelmed by forces within – effectively turning them into another order of knights completely. This sect was so secret, we don't even have a record of their name."

"Now that is spooky," said Charlie. "A band of knights who are there and not there all at the same time. Just imagine what they could do." Bella didn't even need to imagine.

"I want to know how someone got to be accepted into the inner circle of the Knights Templar," said Bella. This was the question that had been brewing in Bella's mind over the last few weeks. Jim leaned over and got out his glasses.

"Now," he started, "if my memory serves me correctly . . ." Jim soon became preoccupied with his scrutiny of the pages, turning forwards, then backwards, then back to the very front of the book before settling on the page he was looking for. "Yes," he said at last. "I thought as much." He turned to a page about three-quarters of the way through the book and started to read, summarizing as he went along.

"Basically," Jim began, "when one of the eight knights of the inner circle died of natural causes, the others would hold a meeting and draw up a list of his successors and then there would be a vote."

"But what if someone who wasn't a member of the group wanted to join them?" Bella interrupted, anxious for a link that might help her understand her father's actions.

"Bella, you astound me," said Annie proudly, and then turned to Jim. "Presumably women weren't allowed to be part of their precious little clan at all."

"I'm afraid not," said Jim.

"Pigs," said Charlie.

"Go on," said Bella.

"Let's see . . ." Jim scrutinized the text. "It seems that if someone was brave enough to challenge one of the elite knights to a duel and won . . ." He fell quiet for a moment while he read ahead. Bella was so beside herself with anticipation, she moved closer and read the text herself.

"Then the other knights would vote on whether to slaughter that person or let him in – depending on what he had to offer them," she said out loud.

"Exactly," said Jim, standing up and giving himself a stretch. "Good guess, Bella." Everyone was giving Bella a questioning look.

"I'm not sure how much of a guess that was, Jim," said Annie, bending down to give Bella a kiss on the forehead. "Bella's quite a one for historical facts."

"She's a bit of a brain box," said Charlie proudly.

But Bella didn't follow any of the idle chitchat going on around her. She was recalling the story Tilahun Alemnew had started to tell her back in Lalibela. "During the war I was ordered on a secret mission to gather information about our enemy's weaponry," he'd started before Mahlet had inter-rupted him. "He was going to tell me that he was a spy," thought Bella. "That he joined the ranks of the enemy to help his side. That's what Yohanis thinks too, only I was too obsessed with my own worries to realize it."

But that wasn't the only conversation on Bella's mind. She recalled how her father had drawn her to the quiet of a tree the day before the summit. She'd been hoping he was going to tell her how much he loved her and all he said was, "Keep your friends and loved ones close to you at all times, but keep your enemies even closer." She'd been so angry with him at the time she hadn't bothered to think about what he'd said.

"So, Father," she thought as the truth behind her father's apparent defection became clearer. "You're attacking them from within." A new dread began to emerge in Bella's mind. "But what if they catch you?" Bella was sure Mr Alemnew had lost his legs as a punishment for his spying.

"Bella?" Charlie beckoned, giving her friend a shake. "Wake up from your trance and let's go and get something to eat. Jim says he's going to buy us chips and cake, remember?"

"Thanks for showing me the book, Uncle Jim," said Bella distractedly.

"You're welcome," said Jim. "Anytime."

Bella was quite subdued over lunch. Luckily, Jim was entertaining Annie and Charlie with anecdotes of museum life and some of their more recent discoveries. For Bella, the realization that her father had taken such control of his destiny on behalf of his cause was as terrifying as it was impressive. She also started to understand more about the kind of battle they were waging.

"I thought the battle referred to in the prophesy meant one big conflict with a quick and clear outcome," she thought, "but it doesn't." She considered the wider use of the term 'battle'. "People battle against all kinds of things that go on for ages," she thought. "We battle against the elements, the opposition, illness and injustice. This battle for a fairer and safer world has hardly even begun."

"Bella," said Annie. "Jim was saying they have some ancient tablets in storage from Nemrud. Wasn't that the place you were reading about the other day?"

"The Forgotten Kingdom," said Bella dreamily.

"Would you like to see them?" asked Jim, mopping up the tomato sauce on his plate with his last chip.

"Yes please, Uncle Jim," said Bella. "When can we go?"

"Hang on, Bella," said Charlie. "We've still got all this chocolate cake to eat first."

After lunch, Jim took them down through two security checks to the vaults beneath the museum.

"Do you know how lucky we are to see these things?" Annie whispered to the girls as they stepped into a large chilly room stacked with boxes and statues wrapped in thick polythene. The room was lit by long fluorescent lights and smelt quite dank.

"I think it's wrong these beautiful things are hidden away here," said Bella. Annie gave her a stern look.

"No, Annie, in many ways Bella is right," said Jim, diplomatically. "In fact, these tablets I'm about to show you are going to be returned to Turkey. Apparently, there's to be a new museum at the base of Mount Nemrud. It's had quite a bit of corporate backing apparently." Bella's body stiffened instantly.

"The Corporation," she thought. "This must be something they want very badly." Bella was impatient to see what they were sending back.

Jim led them to the centre of the room where three very large stone tablets were covered by a thick polyethylene bag. He carefully reached for the end and pulled back the cover, sending up a cloud of dust.

"Wow!" coughed Charlie, admiring the painted symbols that covered each of the three fragments of stone beneath.

"What does it say?" asked Bella eagerly, waving her hands around her face to disperse the dust. As good as she was at reading languages, Bella had never seen an alphabet quite like it.

"It's difficult to interpret," said Jim. "The writing appears to be a cross between Egyptian hieroglyphics and calligraphies from all kinds of ancient languages. To make it even harder to read, the tablets are incomplete." Bella could see that the rocks were jagged and irregular.

"They're broken," said Charlie.

"You're right, Charlie," said Jim. "And it's really frustrating. It's like having three pieces of a ten-piece puzzle." He ran his hand over the text before carrying on. "Apparently, recent excavations in Turkey have unearthed similar tablets. Perhaps, in time, we'll get to see the whole picture, as it were. That's why we're better off sending them back – apart from the moral reasons, obviously."

"But you can't send them back!" Bella protested, imagining what secrets the tablets held and how much harm they could do if they fell into the wrong hands.

"You soon changed your tune," Charlie laughed.

"Mum, I need the camera," said Bella quickly.

"But Bella, I don't know if we're allowed."

Jim looked a little unsure himself.

"Go on then, Bella," he said with a cautious smile. "As long as they're only for you and you don't post them up on the internet, no harm can be done."

Bella took the camera and started to take photographs. She'd been told to trust her instincts and this is exactly what they were telling her to do.

Once she'd checked that the flash had been sufficient to

light her shots, Bella handed the camera back to her mum.

"Thanks, Jim," said Annie. "It's been really lovely to see you. You must come down for Sunday lunch soon and try some of our home-grown vegetables."

"It's a date," said Jim.

"I told you, Bella," Charlie whispered, as they made their way towards the stairs. "The writing is on the wall."

Bella squirmed. "Nah," she said. "They're friends."

Bella, Annie and Charlie walked hand in hand up Oxford Street so they could take in all the wonderful Christmas lights.

"You seem happier now, Bella," said Charlie. "You looked a bit serious over lunch."

"I had something on my mind," said Bella, "but I feel okay now." The realization that her father was alive and in all probability operating as a double agent with the Corporation was deeply worrying but filled Bella with pride. "He's so brave," she thought. "And he fights for what he believes in."

Bella was so close to saying, "Mum, Charlie, I've met my birthfather and he's amazing!" She didn't know how she was going to contain herself.

"What do you want for Christmas, Charlie?" asked Bella as they stopped to admire the window display in the biggest sports shop in town.

"I want my dad to come home," said Charlie. "But I know that's not going to happen." Bella squeezed her friend's hand. "I want my father to come and be with me too," she thought. "And that's not going to happen either." Accepting this made her feel better somehow.

"We want you and your mum to come for Christmas dinner," Bella told Charlie.

"Yes," said Annie. "We'd love it if you could."

The three of them were beaming with happiness. They walked all the way to Leicester Square.

"Come on," said Annie, merrily looking around at all the sparkling billboards on display around the square. "Let's go and see a film."

"Your mum's the best!" Charlie cheered.

When they got home late that afternoon, they found the Quetzal perched on top of a large brown package that had been left on the doorstep.

"This bird seems to have quite a soft spot for you, Bella," said Annie, a little startled by the Quetzal's continuing presence. "Maybe we should adopt him as a family pet."

"Tell me she is joking," said the Quetzal dryly.

"I wish he would stay," thought Bella. "It's comforting being with someone who knows all about me." She knew, however, that London in winter was too cold a place for a tropical bird.

"Hey, Bella, have you been ordering more holiday catalogues on the internet again?" asked Charlie. Bella gave Charlie a stern look.

"Go on," smiled Annie. "I was wondering why we got so many holiday brochures. Take the magazines and that gorgeous bird up to the attic and I'll bring you some juice." The Quetzal fluttered up onto Bella's shoulder.

"A fine judge of plumage, your mum," he twittered. Bella could see now that he'd been trying to peck his way into the parcel.

Bella was ripping the package open even as they climbed up the ladder. She pulled the light switch and tipped all the contents out onto the old Guatemalan chest. What she found took her breath away.

"Bella, it's your pendant!" cried Charlie. "I thought you said it was in your jewellery box." Bella held her precious pendant up to the light. "This is my father's work," she thought, as the sparkling jewels filled her heart with joy. She hunted through the rest of the contents for a note.

"Hurry up," harried the Quetzal, frantically pecking at the folded papers around him. "I haven't got all night."

"This isn't a holiday brochure," said Charlie, kneeling down and unfolding one of the papers. "It looks like a map."

The paper was office-white with a small pencil drawing of Turkey where the province of Adiyaman and a number of historical sights were marked. Both Bella and Charlie were intrigued to see that there was an arrow from a small drawing of Mount Nemrud to a diagram marking out a complex labyrinth of tunnels and tombs.

"Look," said Charlie, picking up the small piece of notepaper she'd spotted on the floor. Bella took the note and opened it up. To her joy she found that it was written in K'iche'. The Quetzal jumped up onto Bella's head for a closer look.

Dear Bella,

I know you're angry with me and very little seems to make any sense, but please keep this map somewhere safe. I've drawn it from memory and not everything about it is complete but I need to know it's safe. Work hard at school and BE PATIENT! Just remember everything I've told you, and that I love you, no matter what happens.

E.S. (your father)
xxx

"Bella, what's all this about?" asked Charlie. Bella gave her friend a long, thoughtful look.

"For goodness sake, don't tell her," squawked the Quetzal.

"I've got so much to tell you, Charlie," said Bella. They were interrupted by footsteps on the ladder.

"So where are we going for our summer holidays then?" asked Annie, appearing at the hatch with a tray of refreshments.

"Turkey!" said Bella quickly, hiding away the contents of her father's parcel. "Let's book it tonight."

Bella asked her mum to come and sit with them for a while and have a look through all the holiday brochures she'd collected. She had no idea what the future held for her and her father, but with Charlie and her mum in her life, the excitement of the fair trade market project, and next year's holiday to Turkey already in the planning, she had an overwhelming sense of optimism.

"I know who I am and I know where I come from," she smiled to herself, proud beyond measure of her Guatemalan parents and their mystical past. "I'm surrounded by people who love me as much as I love them and even without my pendant I have the power to make changes in my world."

As the three of them drank their juice and read the brochures, Bella thought back to the wisdom of her mother, passed on to her by her own, dear father. "Everything that happens in all our yesterdays has its impact on today," she'd said. "But it's what we do with all our tomorrows that determines our destiny."

BELLA BALISTICA AND THE FORGOTTEN KINGDOM

It's the hottest summer on record, and storms and hurricanes are sweeping the country. The Corporation, led by Bella's father, has set the price of oil at an all-time low in a strategy aimed at escalating global warming and promoting their wider business interests. While Bella and her mum try to stem the flood of disasters affecting their lives, the powers of an ancient civilization are being stirred deep within Nemrud Mountain – but to what end? It's the moment of truth for Bella Balistica.

Out soon: *Bella Balistica and the Forgotten Kingdom*, the next book in the Bella Balistica series.

AUTHOR'S NOTE

My travels in Ethiopia were the most vivid and impressionable of any 'safari' I have ever undertaken. Lalibela is truly one of the wonders of the world and the theories and myths surrounding the Ark of the Covenant and the Knights Templar are absolutely compelling. While Bella lives in the real world, her mystical pendant allows her to have fantastical adventures and it's in this spirit that I have manipulated geographic and historical truths to my own ends. The emblem of the Knights Templar was not a creature, a half-man–half-vulture rakah, but the sign of the cross. I've re-jigged the main Ethiopian locations a little so I could use the Simian Mountains while transporting the magnificent medieval fortresses at Gondor to Bahir Dar to avoid any confusion with the Gondor from Tolkien's Lord of the Rings. That aside – the real world feels so magical to me sometimes, I can hardly remember where Bella's fantasy actually took over.

ACKNOWLEDGEMENTS

Thanks to my friend, Tilahun Alemnew, who answered so many queries in my research. Tilahun comes from Lalibela and was my guide for the four days I spent exploring the rock-hewn churches and surrounding mountains. The hospitality of Tilahun's family, and his insight into the town's culture during a time of war for his country, was both unique and exceptionally moving. Without that experience I would not have written this book. While I borrowed Tilahun's name for the story, I need to point out that none of the characters are based on him or any member of his family.

To my readers, Mary Colson and Rebecca Evans, who keep me in check and made exceptionally pertinent observations while reading my early drafts, I again acknowledge a huge debt. Eleise Jones was my copy editor and not only made great technical 'catches' but also many suggestions that I was only too willing to snap up. The support and enthusiasm of my publishers, Patricia Billings and Sedat Turhan at Milet, is inspirational as is the whole talented Milet team. Katie Rundell has done an outstanding job with the design. Thanks also to my agent, Robin Wade, for his unwavering support and guidance and as always and above all, thanks to Charlotte, my wife, who ceaselessly listens to and reads my ideas, inputting at every stage into my work. A big team effort – thank you!

A.G.